What Kind Of Love Is This?

Captivating A Boss

Tina J

Copyright 2018

More Books by Tina J

A Thin Line Between Me & My Thug 1-2
I Got Luv for My Shawty 1-2
Kharis and Caleb: A Different kind of Love 1-2
Loving You is a Battle 1-3
Violet and the Connect 1-3
You Complete Me
Love Will Lead You Back
This Thing Called Love
Are We in This Together 1-3
Shawty Down to Ride For a Boss 1-3
When a Boss Falls in Love 1-3
Let Me Be The One 1-2
We Got That Forever Love
Ain't No Savage Like The One I got 1-2
A Queen & Hustla 1-2 (collab)
Thirsty for a Bad Boy 1-2
Hasaan and Serena: An Unforgettable Love 1-2
We Both End Up With Scars
Caught up Luvin a beast 1-3
A Street King & his Shawty 1-2
I Fell for the Wrong Bad Boy 1-2 (collab)
Addicted to Loving a Boss 1-3
All Eyes on the Crown 1-3
I Need that Gangsta Love 1-2 (collab)
Still Luvin' a Beast 1-2
Creepin' With The Plug 1-2
I Wanna Love You 1-2
Her Man, His Savage 1-2
When She's Bad, I'm Badder 1-3
Marco & Rakia 1-3
Feenin' for a Real One 1-3
A Kingpin's Dynasty 1-3
What Kind Of Love Is This?

Khloe

"Are you almost finished Khloe?" My mom asked and strolled in the kitchen. I lived on my own but since she's always here, it never felt like it.

"Ma, I just started." She rolled her eyes and walked out. How the hell she rushing me and I'm the one who just got off work?

"Well hurry the fuck up. I'm hungry." I sucked my teeth and continued cooking the spaghetti.

"Why don't you take her ass home!" Luna sarcastically said in my ear. She couldn't stand my mother and the feelings were definitely mutual. Sometimes they'd argue so bad, it's a struggle tryna keep them from coming to blows. I'm not saying Luna should disrespect my mother at any time but I understand why she does. I avoid confrontation with her as much as possible because she is my mother but it's definitely hard. My mom is very judgmental, petty, disrespectful and doesn't give two shits about hurting someone's feelings.

4

"My dad is at work and she hates to be alone. You know that already." I didn't understand why Luna even asked because we've gone through this a thousand times. When my father's working, my mom is here and it's been this way for a very long time.

"Girl bye! Your dad gets off in an hour. By the time she takes the forty-minute drive, he'll be home shortly after."

"It's ok Luna."

"No it's not Khloe. Mother or not, she is using you." I rolled my eyes and placed the biscuits in the oven.

I stood there with the phone to my ear listening to Luna go in about my mom. See, my parents lived paycheck to paycheck and me; I'm doing just fine. I graduated top of my class with a Master's degree in Business and Management, along with a minor in accounting. I loved working with numbers so much, I became an accountant for a few businesses in the area as a side hustle. I made very good money and both of my parents knew it. My dad was extremely happy while my mother; well she's another story. It's not that she wasn't happy, it's more of, she wanted what I had.

I have my own black card, a brand-new Mercedes GLS truck and my own three-bedroom townhouse. I could've owned a single-family home but then I'd have to find someone to mow the lawn, shovel the snow, and let's not discuss any maintenance issues that may arise. When you're in a townhome or condo, all of that is included in your association fees.

Anyway, I had a shopping habit and regardless of how much things may cost, if I wanted it, I'd get it. My mother made sure to accompany me on any and every shopping trip possible; knowing I'd purchase things for her. My mom envied me, even though she won't say it. My dad did ask me to stop because he felt some type of way because he couldn't afford the lifestyle I was making her accustomed to.

However, my mom would make me feel like shit if I did. She'd say I didn't love her and then go on about how she gave up this and that to raise me; blah, blah, blah. I respected the hell outta my parents for sacrificing what they have to make sure I was ok. But I was very smart and had so many scholarships, they never came outta pocket for anything regarding college. Shit, I didn't even have student loans and a bitch was more than happy about it, but not my mom. She'd somehow find a way to say my success is attributed to her being my mom.

For instance, she'd say shit like, *"You know, if I didn't let you sit up all night studying, you wouldn't be a smart as you are. Or, I was going to get an abortion so you should be happy about living. Oh, the best one is, its time to take care of me for the next eighteen years since I had to waste my life doing it for you.* Things to make you wanna smack the fuck outta her. Luna has witnessed it on plenty of occasions and would call her out on it often, hence the reason they don't get along.

"I don't wanna get into it with you right now Luna."

"Khloe I understand, but stop letting her make you think you're obligated to do things for her. Hell, her ass has a job and when's the last time she took you out to eat? Or offered to take you shopping."

"You know they don't have it like that."

7

"Not the point. Chili's, Red Lobster and those places are not expensive. Yet, you continue taking her to all these seafood and expensive spots. Let's not discuss the clothes you buy her."

"I know." I ran my hand through my hair as I stood in the kitchen. I loved Luna like my sister and I respected her thoughts but sometimes I didn't wanna hear it. I don't know if it's because she was right and I was in denial or because its still my mom.

"All I'm saying K, is put her on a budget if you plan on taking care of her."

"A budget?"

"You're the one pretending she's your child so treat her like one. Give her an allowance or something."

"She's gonna be mad."

"Who the fuck cares?" I could hear the anger in her voice. I understood where her and my father were coming from but its hard when she makes me feel guilty every chance she gets.

"Look, I gotta get ready for tonight. You still coming right?" She asked and I stared at my mom in disgust, as she sat in my living room with her feet up and not a care in the world.

"I guess."

"Bitch, I will come snatch your ass up."

"My mom wants to.-" I tried to get out but she cut me off.

"OH HELL NO! We've been planning this all week. Your mom needs to go home." I blew my breath out.

"I'll meet you there around ten."

"Fine!" I said but wasn't really sure if I still wanted to go.

"Don't make me come get you." We laughed and I disconnected the call.

"About time you hung up with her ugly ass." She walked back in the kitchen holding her wine glass. I swear, all she did after work is come here until my father got home and complain, complain, complain. I know, I should put my foot down but I'm trying my hardest to respect the fact that she's

9

my mother. My mom claimed to love me but I felt like she only did when it benefitted her.

"Not tonight ma." I took the biscuits out, along with the salad and made her a plate. She sat down and stared at me. I became uncomfortable because if she stared, it meant her words were about to be deadly. She had a mean streak towards me outta this world at times, which is why I hope she's gone before I leave.

Here's your food." She picked the fork up and started to eat. I made my plate and did the same. Each minute passing, I waited for the negative comments and they didn't come until I was about to leave.

"Are you really going out looking like that?" I stopped midway down the steps because it's like she waited for me to get ready just to be mean. At least if she did it before I got dressed, I'd have time to get over it.

"Ma you were supposed to be gone a long time ago." After dinner she said she was leaving, so I retreated upstairs and started to get ready. I was already running late because after dinner, I had to clean my kitchen and received no help at all.

"I'm leaving now. Your father worked late and..." She looked me up and down again and turned her face up. I glanced at my outfit to make sure nothing was wrong.

It was a spandex black cat suit and I wore a black laced pair of peep toe red bottom, ankle boots. I didn't care for the Louboutin shoes, due to how narrow they were and my feet weren't gonna squeeze in them anyway. But the ankle boots fit perfectly. I had on silver accessories to match and a silver Gucci belt that was hard to find but I got it. My hair was flowing down my back and my makeup was flawless as always. A bitch never stepped out looking a mess, whether it was for work or leisure.

"Don't get gang raped." My mouth flew open as she opened the door. I couldn't believe those words left her mouth.

"Close your mouth and keep your legs closed."

"Why would you say that?" She turned to look at me and it was at that very moment, I knew not only did she envy me, but jealousy was staring me in my face.

11

"You got all that hanging out and you got gook on your face. Men will assume you're a prostitute and you know what happens after that." She had the nerve to kiss my cheek and close the door.

I fell back on the couch. I could feel the tears welling in my eyes and my stomach started doing flips. Whenever I'd get upset, I would have to shit something serious. The doctor said, I had Irritable Bowel Syndrome and any stress or being upset would trigger it. I picked my phone up to call Luna and cancel but someone knocked at my door. I opened it and she knew right away my mother said some fucked up shit.

"Not tonight Khloe." She closed the door and walked over to me.

"Here." She dug in her purse, grabbed me a few Tums and made me take them.

"I don't wanna know what she said because its only gonna piss me off and make me wanna go to her house." She grabbed my hand and led me to the door.

"Spring break is in two weeks and we're going away. And before you ask, HELL FUCKING NO, your mother is not

12

coming." I busted out laughing and locked the door. That's the thing about Luna I loved the most. She could always make me feel better in a bad situation.

"Why did you come? I thought we were meeting at the club." I asked and sat inside her GMC Acadia truck.

"Bitch, I knew that hag was gonna say something to make you upset." She pulled out the complex and we drove to the club to have fun.

I didn't wanna say it but I believe its time to give my mom a piece of my mind and distance myself away from her. Unfortunately, the last time I tried she kept my father away with lies and I'm a daddy's girl to the max. I was so afraid of it happening again, I allowed her to treat me bad. *The things we tolerate to stay in someone's life.*

"You can place everything in those drawers, in totes, boxes or black garbage bags. I don't really give a fuck." I told the three guys from the moving company.

"Do you want any of these shoes and purses in a tote or will the misses be picking them up?" I glanced around the four-bedroom house I had my ex of three years living in and realized she had more shit than I thought.

"That too can go in a bag." I walked in the bedroom and saw all types of clothing with tags on it. Something told me to look down and there were a pair of men sneakers under the bed. Now me, I wear Jordan's for leisure and nothing but Tom Ford and other name brand stuff when I go out. Therefore, whoever shit this was isn't mine because they were pumas. I'm not hating on a nigga because people can only afford what they could. However, don't step to me like you're taking my woman and can't provide for her like I could.

For anyone who's lost, let me start from the beginning. My name is Ryan *Risky* Wells, and I'm a funeral home director by day and killa by night. If you're wondering; absolutely, I bury the same niggas I kill. That's the beauty of it. To know, I'm the one who took the person's life and then had to put them in the ground was an adrenaline rush for me and I couldn't get enough.

Don't ask me why the families came to me after a loved one was killed because it was other funeral homes but I'm the only African American owner, which could be a reason. The way I put them to rest always had people in awe. I'm talking about having pall bearers doing a dance as they came down the aisle and everything. Yea, I learned that move from this guy in St. Louis who buried a lot of people too. He had a show on TV and him and his boys had a banging ass set for the dead. Of course, mine wasn't exactly the same but believe you me; whether I killed you or not, your body was laid to rest nice.

I remember when I first came up with the idea to go into this business. I was getting outta the game and wanted to wash my money like most Kingpins. People thought I was crazy and the only ones who had faith in my vision was my mom, Lacey, who is Raina's mom and one of my boy's

Waleed. Lamar, who is Lacey's twin wasn't beat and actually mad I stepped away from the drug game. I think he was more pissed I handed everything over to Waleed and not him.

It wasn't personal but Waleed was my right-hand man since we were kids and Lamar was only around because of his sister. Plus, the connect didn't wanna work with him. He said Lamar was sneaky and had a deceiving way about him. Don't ask me what he meant but I respected his choice. I still consult with Waleed if he has questions about anything and if he needs help, I'm right there. He's been doing his thing for the last seven years and I can honestly say, he's making a lotta money.

Anyway, back to who I am. I'm twenty-nine years old with a twelve-year-old daughter named Raina. She is a daddy's girl, spoiled to the core and unfortunately, lost her mother at the age of five to gun violence. I was devastated because she was the woman I planned on marrying.

The week of her funeral was hard for me because I am the one who performed the service. I sat in the room the first night we got her, for hours crying and asking God why he had to take her. It wasn't until my mom came and said my daughter wanted me that I finally got it together. Regardless of how much I needed my girl to come back, my daughter needed me more. Needless to say, after the funeral a lotta bodies dropped and I was a very busy and paid man.

"Yo, what the fuck going on here?" Waleed came in stepping over stuff on the floor.

"You know I'm throwing her ass out."

"Oh yea, I forgot. But what's all this?" He pointed to some of the bags.

"Getting rid of everything. I have someone who wants to buy this place so I need to get this shit outta here and we both know, she won't lift a fucking finger to help." I owned a few properties as well to keep me busy when I'm not working with the dead.

"Make that money. Fuck it."

"You know it. What's up with you?" I asked and continued checking the place to make sure none of my things were here.

"I have to fly to Miami in two weeks. You down?" He sat on the bed and looked on the ground.

"Who's busted ass sneakers are these?"

"Man, you know they're not mine."

"Damn, Ronny couldn't even get a nigga who wore Jordan's or at least Adidas?" He referred to my ex Veronica. We called her Ronny for short because she hated her name.

"Guess not. Do you know this nigga had the nerve to ask if we were broken up yet when I saw him at the store?" I had a feeling Ronny was doing something she had no business but to find out she cheated blew my mind.

"Say word?"

"Word. Then he claimed to be in love and would treat her better. You know the bullshit they try and run on you when they fucking your girl. Don't even ask how he knew who I was."

"Damn, he got balls."

"I guess she threw the pussy on him." I said and shrugged my shoulders. then went in the closet to get my money out the safe.

I opened it and there were at least five stacks missing. I glanced back at Waleed and he shook his head. He knew how much money I kept here and didn't have to say a word to understand what I was about to say. Ronny had the combination to the safe because sometimes she wanted to shop and I'd tell her to take some. Who knew, she'd take more when I supplied her with any and everything she needed. In my eyes, that's stealing and I'm glad we're through.

"What's going on? Why are you moving my things?" We heard and I stood up.

"We were paid to do so." One of the guys said and I could hear her stomping up the steps.

"RISKYYYYYYYYYY!" She shouted and Waleed sat back grinning. He always got a kick outta other people's problems.

"What's going on?" She tossed her purse at my boy and stood in front of me.

"What's going on is we're over."

"Over? For what?" She looked around the room at all her things in bags and totes.

"When did you start stealing from me?"

"I...I..." She tried to get her words out.

19

"Oh hell no Risky. If she stuttering that means she's about to lie." She gave Waleed a deadly look.

"I only took some to go away. You told me to take what I needed."

"Ronny, I purchased the plane tickets for you, gave you ample money to shop and I always give you spending money so why did you take it?" She couldn't say a word.

"You're leaving me over this."

"Awww shit now. Its about to get real good."

"Waleed, why are you here? Don't you have a bitch to give a disease or baby too?"

"Bitch, my dick stay clean. I wish, I would fuck a bitch raw." She sucked her teeth.

"I know you only said it because I made your dumb ass friend suck my dick with a condom on. Then she goes out, catches something and tries to call me. She better call that nigga who gave it to her." Ronny gave him the finger as I scrolled through the messages on my phone.

"Risky, what's going on?" I saw how watery her eyes were getting. I handed her my phone, grabbed a duffle bag and began putting the remaining money in it. I only kept money over here because sometimes I didn't feel like going to the bank or taking it to my house and put it in my own safe. Maybe I should've taken it home if she was stealing. I wonder how many times she's done it and I didn't notice?

"Oh shit baby. Fuck me just like that."

"He was giving you the business huh Ronny?" Waleed was pissing her off even more. See the video I showed her, is of a guy who approached me in the store a few days ago and mentioned he was with my woman. I was unsure of who he was talking about because I was only with Veronica and I know damn well he couldn't be speaking of her.

Low and behold, he showed me a photo of her first with him and they were hugging. It wasn't nothing to worry about because she was friendly like that. However, when he showed me the video of them fucking in the exact bed Waleed is sitting on now, I was done. At first, I was gonna beat his ass for recording her until her stupid ass started performing for the camera. I couldn't believe she allowed him to catch her slipping.

21

"Risky, let me explain."

"Explain what?" I zipped the bag and place it on my shoulder.

"Is that you in the video?"

"Yea, is it Ronny. I didn't see it but it sure sounds like you." She threw the lotion off the dresser at him.

"Risky, she still violent huh?" Ronny had a crazy streak about her when it came to me. I guess after a few years any woman would.

"Is that you?" She put her head down and I tilted it back and forced her to look at me.

"Then you had the nerve to bring him in this house." I pointed to the Puma's on the floor.

"The same house I brought you. The one, I fuck you in and the same one, my daughter comes to sometimes. You were on some other shit." She put her head back down because she was caught.

"I gave you any and everything you wanted. You helped me raise my daughter for the last four years and

22

marriage was in the future for us but you blew it to be a porn star."

"Risky, I was drunk and Dora told me we were going…"

"DORA!" I shouted and Waleed and I both looked at her like she was stupid.

"That bitch is messy and has a loose pussy. Why would you even entertain anything she said?" I waited for her to answer because if she did anything with Dora, it couldn't be good.

"She asked if he could come over and we were drinking and having a good time. Honestly, I don't remember that night." It was only a few days ago because I saw her leave in the outfit the night in question. It was the same one in the video, right before she got naked. I took my daughter to the movies that night and stayed home, which is why I wasn't her when this bullshit took place.

"How could you not remember? You're performing for the camera." What she said next, had me floored.

"I took some ecstasy pills and.-" I dropped the bag and threw her against the wall.

"What the fuck I tell you about doing that dumb shit?" I had my hand around her throat.

Her and Dora were always careless and sloppy when they went out, which is why I didn't really like her to go with her alone. The last time they did, Dora had Ronny try molly and she ended up in the hospital. She also suffered a miscarriage. Neither of us even knew she was pregnant, which hurt more because we were trying for a baby at one point but after that, I refused to give her my seeds. The only way she'd get a baby outta me, is if we were married.

"Risky calm down. You're about to kill her." I could hear Waleed in my ear but I was so mad she allowed that dumb friend of hers to get her caught up in some bullshit that I didn't wanna let go.

"Let go bro." He had to pry my hands off her. By the time he did, she passed out and I stepped right over her to leave. I bent down to her ear. I wasn't sure if she could hear me or not.

"Don't hit my line no more and if you even think about going near Raina, I'll fucking kill you." She may have helped me raise her but if she's being carless and shit by taking pills, I can't take the chance of her having my daughter over and she have it lying around.

"Oh, and once these movers leave there will be a padlock on this door. I'm selling it." I stood and left her laying there. All the years we've been together, she's never done anything remotely stupid as she did, taking pills. Her and Dora been friends for a long time but ever since she started fucking with Lamar, she's been on some other shit and dumb ass Veronica went right along with it.

"Damn bro, I'm sorry. I didn't know she was doing all that." Waleed knew about the molly because he came to the hospital but I found out the same time he did about the ecstasy and the shit burned me up.

"Its all good. What day we leaving for Florida?"

"Two weeks."

"Aight. Hit me with the date so I can let my mom's and Raina know." We slapped hands.

"You think the dead people will be fine without you for a few days?"

"Fuck you, yo." He started laughing.

"I'm just saying."

"Whatever. I'll see you at the airport." We gave each other a pound and went our separate ways.

****

"Hey daddy. Is Ronny with you?" I gave her a hug and smiled. My daughter was my everything. She resembled her mom a lot and sometimes it made me upset thinking about what happened.

"Nah."

"Good." I didn't say anything and went in the kitchen with my mom. Ronny and Raina definitely had a love/ hate relationship.

"Hey ma. Let me talk to you two right quick." She hung up the phone with whomever she spoke to and sat at the table with me and Raina.

"You ok?" I ran my hand down my face and blew my breath. I was in my feelings about Veronica sleeping around

26

and taking pills. It had me asking myself if she was addicted or really knew what she was doing. Whatever the case, we were over for sure.

"Veronica and I are no longer together and.-"

"THANK YOU JESUS! I PRAYED ON THIS." My mom wasn't even religious, yet she talking about she prayed on it.

"Really ma?"

"That woman is vindictive and put on one heck of a show around you." I gave her a crazy look. My mom has never spoken ill of Ronny so I'm a little confused of why the sudden change.

"Raina, can you give us a minute." I asked her and she stood.

"Daddy, I don't have to go over her house, do I?"

"No and if she comes to your school, do not leave with her. Call me right away." I thought she would question it but its like she didn't care. I stood up and grabbed a piece of cake off the counter.

"Son, I didn't wanna tell you this but Veronica is not who she seemed to be."

"Elaborate." I took a bite of the cake.

"I caught her a few times saying mean things to Raina." The cake fell out my hand.

"Come again." She put her hand on mine.

"She'd call Raina fat and tell her she couldn't eat what normal kids ate because it would make her big. Son, she had Raina sticking her finger down her throat."

"WHATTTTT?" I jumped out my seat and started pacing.

"Calm down Ryan." She never referenced me to my street name. She hated it, even though I got it from her.

She told me growing up, I was always willing to risk my life to help others. For instance, she said, one day a small kid was running in the street and a car was coming. I ran out, snatched the kid and fell on the side of the road. We were both safe but we hit our heads and had concussions. There were a ton of other times I did wild shit as well and don't let her speak on my street life because that alone is risky in her eyes.

"Why didn't you tell me? And my daughter isn't fat." I peeked at her in the living room watching television. Raina was a little chunky for regular twelve-year olds but I never paid it any mind because I'm sure being in sports and other activities will make it fall off. She was already in soccer, cheerleading for pop warner and was the star player on the girls' middle school basketball team. Her legs were thick and so was her upper body. She had a small stomach but to me she was big boned and even if she were fat, who cares? How the fuck was this bitch calling my daughter names behind my back?

"Why didn't Raina tell me?"

"I asked her the same and son she was scared."

"Scared of what?"

"You left her alone with Veronica all the time. She was worried you wouldn't believe her, tell Veronica and she'd beat her."

"How long has this been going on?"

"I don't know."

"You don't know!"

29

"Ryan, I didn't know at first and once she told me, I promised to keep her secret. Why do you think every time you went outta town and didn't take Veronica, I made it my business to have her stay here? I refused to let her stay there."

"But there were times when I did leave her."

"Look." She stood and came to me.

"I understand you're upset but don't bring it up to her. She thinks you're ashamed of her because that bitch told her you wouldn't take her anywhere if she was too big." I put my head down in shame. How the hell did I miss Ronny mistreating my daughter? There were no signs and I damn sure didn't hear Raina vomiting or anything.

"She's gonna need to speak to someone." She patted my shoulder.

"Why?"

"Veronica may not be able to get to her like before but her self-esteem is down. The kids call her names at school due to her weight and I'm scared she may do something harmful. You know kids are killing themselves for being bullied."

"Fuck! I'm gonna kill that bitch." I tried to grab my keys but she snatched them out my hand.

"Relax. You're no longer with her and as long as we get her help, she should be fine." I nodded and went to sit with my daughter. She was on the couch with a pair of beats in her ear. If my mom didn't mention the shit with Veronica, I'd think she had no care in the world.

Unfortunately, she probably had a lot on her mind. I moved her hair behind her ear and kissed her cheek. I thought about her mom and how she struggled with her weight too after giving birth. She was always a size eight but after delivering she went to a size twelve. She didn't have a stomach but her hips and ass were thick. To be honest, I loved it but I know women have a complex about shit and I pray my daughter doesn't grow up feeling the same.

Khloe

"This is the worst spring break ever." I told Luna as we sat in the bar at the hotel. We were at a resort in Hawaii for a week and it rained every day since we've been here and that's four days. We had three more days left in this washed out place and I prayed it would get better.

"I know right. Do you wanna leave and finish our vacation in Miami?" Our spring break was to start in Hawaii for seven days and the last four would be spent in the sunshine state of Florida. We took one of these vacations every year around this time and this is the worst one ever.

"It may not be any rooms available."

"Girl please. We may be going a little early but my dad purchased our room in the most expensive hotel in Miami. Those college kids and other spoiled brats aren't staying in anything remotely expensive as us." I had to laugh at Luna because she was a piece of work. Talking about someone being spoiled, she is the poster child for it.

Her dad and uncle, run the Mexican cartel out in Mexico and ran a few states here too. They have thousands of people working under them; they have to be billionaires by now. Oh, and let's not mention the amount of money he allows her to run through daily. That girl can buy a thousand dollars' worth of things today, swear she doesn't have anything to wear, and go shopping again tomorrow. I thought, I was a shopaholic but she has me beat.

She always had to have at least three bodyguards wherever she went and if she tried to make someone her man, he had to go through a bunch of tests from her pops. Which is why, she snuck around and we did our thing on vacation. I have to admit over the last few years of us going on these vacations, we had a few one-night stands. Say what you want but we didn't have a man and as long as we were protected, who cares?

You see, Luna and I aren't your average Instagram, Facebook, or Snap Chap models. Actually, we're both on the big size but we don't call ourselves a BBW. Although, men did seem to call us that on occasion. It didn't really bother us because other than our weight, we both had pretty faces, our own place, car, job and could hold our own when it came to putting a bitch or nigga in their place.

Luna was a Mexican American with that caramel complexion and long black hair. Her chest had to be a 40 DD and the bottom half of her was thicker than thick and toned up. She didn't have a huge stomach but she had enough for a man to grab on, if he wanted to. At five foot five and two hundred pounds, I guess she would be considered big. People often tell her she resembles Selena Gomez, just on the heavy side. Saying someone had a pretty face to be big is not a compliment, as some would think.

I'm five foot four and about a hundred and ninety five pounds. My parents are both black and I was blessed to have a big ass and huge hips. Unfortunately, my lazy ass don't work out so I can see the cellulite and dimples in more than I care to admit. My arms are chunky and stomach is flat because regardless of how huge my legs were, I refused to have a big stomach. Plus, I could lay down in my bed and do crunches. *I told you I was lazy.* My hair is long but I hate doing it, therefore; I kept it in a weave so I can wake up and go. The beautician set aside an appointment for me once a week and took very good care of me.

"I guess you're right. Let's bounce and get our party on."

"Bitch! You know I'm finding you a man when we get there." I rolled my eyes as she went on and on about getting me one. Even if she couldn't have a boyfriend she always wanted me to have one. She said, I was gonna die alone and she wasn't having it.

"Luna, I don't want any man. Shit, Marcus put me through so much, I've had enough drama to last me a lifetime. I damn sure don't need a new one to give me more." I pressed the elevator and stepped on, with her behind me.

Marcus was my ex-boyfriend. He and I, were college sweethearts or so I thought. We met at freshman orientation and dated the entire four years of school. He was the man I desperately wanted to marry, have kids and ride off in the sunset with. This man could do no wrong in my eyes, that is until the day of graduation where all my dreams with him were crushed.

"Marcus, really?" Some woman yelled as he was still on his knee proposing. I had just walked outside to where everyone was after receiving my diploma. My parents, cousins and his family were all in attendance.

"Khloe, will you marry me?" He continued as if this woman wasn't charging towards us with a baby in her arms and a big stomach.

"You're gonna marry some bitch, knowing we have two kids together." The air escaped my body and I could hear the gasps leaving everyone's mouth.

"Bitch, move." He pushed her back and came over to me.

"Those aren't my kids Khloe and.-"

"They're not, huh?" She handed me a piece of paper and it read 99.99999% clear as day.

"What the fuck is that?"

"Something told me you would pull this bullshit, so when you were sleep one night, I swabbed your mouth and did

36

a DNA test." I could see the hate radiating off his body.

Marcus has never been violent towards me but the way he

stared at this woman, had me scared for her.

"Marcus, I'm not going to pretend this isn't hurting

because it is. However, I won't participate in being ratchet or

ghetto in front of our family. I will ask you to remove yourself

from me and take her with you." See, I had a little properness

in me but I can be ghetto as hell too. My dad always told me to

let it out when necessary.

"K, it was a mistake and.-"

"Is that child in her stomach yours?" When he put his

head down the tears began to fall. To know he got her

pregnant once is one thing but to do it again, is like stabbing

me in the chest over and over.

"K, we can move past this. Come on baby. You weren't

giving it up and I needed to get my dick wet." I smacked the

shit outta him. Not only did he break my virginity the previous

year, he knew it took me a while to get comfortable in having

sex. The reason being is, it was painful at first and it would

take me a few weeks to wanna try it again. This went on for a

37

few months but once I became comfortable, we were like porn stars; which is why I got on birth control right away.

"It takes nine months to carry a child and that baby looks to be at least six months old. Her stomach is out there so I'm guessing she's about four or five now. You had to be sleeping with this woman for over two years, am I right?" The woman shook her head with a smirk on her face.

"Marcus you are dead to me."

"Khloe, get back here." He came running behind me and the chick handed her child over to his mother. The kid didn't cry or anything, which most do when they don't know someone.

"You knew about the child?" I asked her and she put her head down.

"I thought you loved me as your own daughter."

"Khloe, I do and always will. What he did has nothing to do with me." She had the nerve to say. I know he's her son but damn they really had me out here looking like a fool.

"You're right but you should've made him tell me or you could have. All the times, I've been on the phone with you

discussing my future with him. I've spent the night at your

house with him and even been there for holidays and this entire

time you knew." I could no longer stomach any of the people

here.

"Let's go sunshine." Its what my dad called me. He

held my hand as we walked to the car and I could hear Luna

cursing Marcus and anyone else out who knew. She was my

ride or die chick and once her craziness kicked in, watch out.

"You ok?" My dad looked at me from the front seat.

My mom had a smirk on her face as if she were getting a kick

outta me being in pain. I heard the door open and Luna

jumped in.

"Dad, how could he?" I leaned my head on the door.

"Honey, men have a lot of secrets and unfortunately, he

kept this quiet. Whoever the chick is must've known about you

because she picked a hell of a day to pop up, don't you think?"

I had to agree.

I was upset, hurt, humiliated and also relieved.

Relieved because had I accepted his proposal, gone through

with the marriage and found out about the kids later, I don't know what I would've done. That was five years ago and I

haven't been in a relationship since then. I may have had my

one-night stands but I wasn't interested in having a man. I'm

sure he'd disappoint me eventually, and I'm good on my own.

"Chica, you ok?' Luna pulled me off the elevator.

"Yea. When you brought up Marcus, the memories

came back and I started reminiscing."

"Girl, don't waste your memories on the past. He isn't

worth it. Anyway, let's get it poppin bitch." She started

throwing things in her luggage and so did I. This trip may have

been a drag but I'm sure Miami will have a lot more going on

and I can't wait.

****

"Damn, its' hot out here." I fanned myself with one of

the papers I picked up off the desk inside the airport. It was a

lot of people and I hated it. We could've flown on her parents'

jet but she wanted to be normal, as she says. I bet her ass

regretting it now because she was complaining more than me.

"Bitch, you know we big girls and the heat don't get

along with us." I told her and she we both started laughing.

"We damn sure taking the jet back home. I'm not built for hard labor." She had the nerve to say.

"Hard labor. Luna, you ain't doing shit."

"Bitch, I'm fanning myself. I have people to do that for me." I fell out laughing.

"Don't laugh because when your ass comes over, you damn sure use the staff too."

"What the fuck ever. That's what they there for?" I said because they were. I tried not to use them but whenever I went to her house, they would pop up right when you would do something. Its like they were waiting to be told what to do.

"Exactly bitch. Now let's go get some dick or at least stalk some."

"I fucking hate you Luna."

"I know."

We made our way to the baggage claim and waited for our things. I glanced around and there were some sexy men in the airport. Some were with women and others were most likely down here to fuck and bounce. Hell, its what most spring breakers did anyway. I would be a fool to expect anything other than that.

These days men only wanna have sex and move on. Its like they're allergic to the word *relationship* and *monogamous.* Maybe if we had more committed men, there wouldn't be so many single moms. The crazy part is, women seem to be doing the same thing now and it only makes me think this world is only gonna get worse.

"Yo, what the fuck?" I yelled out at some dude who tried to jump in front of me and take the cab. After Khloe and I grabbed our bags, I knew it would be hard to get one.

"What the fuck, what?" He towered over me and I put my hand up for my bodyguards to stay put. I didn't want them taking me anywhere and my dad told them only intervene when necessary. I stared his fine ass up and down and had he not been rude, I may have bedded his ass. Those pretty brown eyes, the gold grill and the bow legs did something to a bitch. I may be of Mexican descent but I loved me some African American men.

"You see our sexy asses about to get in this cab and…" He started looking around and had me doing the same. I thought someone was about to run up on us or something.

"Who you looking for?" I asked and he peeked around me.

"I'm looking for the sexy women who were about to get in this cab because you sure as hell ain't one. I mean your face is decent, but you got way too much thickness going on to be called sexy."

"Motherfucker, did you just call me fat?" I had my hands on my hips. When a man said too much thickness, it usually meant you're too big to be called slim thick or thickum and most likely, called you fat in a nice way.

"What you think?" He gave me the *duh* face.

"Let me tell you something nigga." I had my index finger in his face. He smacked my hand and I stepped back a little.

"You may be a tad bit cute and your swag is on point but your tiny ass dick couldn't handle a woman like me, which is why you came for my weight. You see niggas like you want a BBW or plus size woman as you call us but too scared of what your friends may think. Let me be the first to tell you." I walked up closer and grabbed his dick. His shit felt thick and long but it could be the jeans. Some men wear basketball shorts and boxers under their jeans too, so I can't say for sure if it's really big or not.

"You may be working with a little something, something but you're disrespectful as fuck. Now move so we can get in." I squeezed harder and he bent over in pain.

"Put our things in the trunk please." I told the cab driver and he did what I asked with a smirk on his face. K, got in the car and closed the door.

"I hope we don't have an issue after this." I squeezed harder, kissed his cheek and jumped in the back seat. By the time he composed himself we were pulling off. *Stupid motherfucker.* I turned around and some guy was standing next to him cracking up. That's what the fuck he gets.

"Bitchhhhh, are you crazy?"

"Fuck that K. I'm tired of these sexy ass men thinking because we're big boned they can say what they want. I may not be a skinny ass model showing my body off but I have feelings too and if I'm not disrespecting you, then I expect the same in return."

"I get it Luna but we're far from home."

"And we have security."

"Girl you crazy." Is all she could say because she knew I was right. I leaned my head back on the seat and waited for the cab to take us to our destination.

Once we arrived, the bellhop came out to assist with our bags. I had my father call ahead and they had the room on the twentieth floor waiting. It was a penthouse of course because I only rested in the best places. Khloe, hated to be anywhere higher than the second because she was scared of heights but stayed looking out the windows. She said her heart would palpitate each time but the views are always to die for. I handed the guy a tip and closed the door.

"Let's take a nap and hit the strip tonight." She agreed and both of us went into separate rooms. I looked at the clock and it was only five so I set the alarm for eight to get up and get ready. Miami is a party city so even if we went out early, we'd still have fun.

****

The alarm went off and a bitch was more tired from the nap, then I was before going to sleep. I called Khloe's phone to wake her up and hopped in the shower.

"Ok bitch. I see you." I said to Khloe when she came out the bedroom.

She had on a red half shirt that read sexy and some black denim jeans. As you can tell, black is her favorite color. Her stomach was flat as fuck and I hated my ass for not taking the time out to get mine the same. She wore a red belt and some red heels. I had on a white halter shirt that came above my ass, some dark blue fitted jeans and a pair of black stilettos. My titties were big but I had bras specially made to make them perky. Not only that, I was getting a reduction in a couple months. These things are killing my back and while men may love them, I don't.

"Bitch, you cute too."

"You ain't got to tell me." I started twerking. We may be big boned, thick, BBW's or whatever men called us but we were some bad bitches. I grabbed the room key, my phone and we headed out the door.

"Are you sure I look ok?" This is the only thing I hated about K. Her mom put her down so much, she became self-conscious and would ask me a thousand times how she looked.

I'd have to get her tipsy right away and she'd stop. I think being around skinny bitches did it too. They always had something to say and she'd get in her feelings, where I'd curse them out.

"You're fine." We stepped off the elevator and the few men in the lobby stared hard as hell. One in particular stood out and I grabbed Khloe's hand and started walking fast.

"What the hell? Why are we speed walking?" I turned around and saw that nigga standing at the door. I gave him the finger and he mouthed the words *fuck you.*

"Bitch, that was the nigga from the airport." She turned around.

"Don't look."

"Why you running though?"

"Ugh you do remember I grabbed his dick, squeezed it and talked shit. He still looks mad."

"That's what your tough ass gets. Always bothering someone." She shook her head and I mushed her in it.

"I know you better not had messed my hair up." I sucked my teeth and we hopped in the black SUV my bodyguards were in. I didn't wanna have them take me but we didn't rent a car and I refused to wait for an Uber.

We pulled up to some strip club and the line was wrapped around the corner. Mind you, it was only ten at night. One of the guards stepped out, went to the door and gestured for us to come. The bouncer moved the red rope and had a bottle girl whisked us to VIP. The area was sectioned off and had two couches in it. There was a small hookah area and a damn stripper pole. This must be where most of the ballers frequented and had their own strip shows.

"Can I get you ladies something to drink?" The waitress asked and we placed our order.

"I need the bathroom." I could tell by her face that she had to shit.

"K, did you take the Prilosec!"

"Yea but look at all these skinny bitches. Maybe we should go to a club that isn't so high maintenance."

"Fuck those bitches. Look, I'll go to the bathroom with you but we're not leaving." I pointed for her to walk. My bodyguard stepped out the way and once we got in, it was no

49

one in there. I ended up using it myself and waited for K to emerge from her stall.

"Bitch, Risky got me fucked up." Some chick said coming in. She was gorgeous if I say so myself. The exact type of woman Khloe felt self-conscious around. I heard the toilet flush and she came out.

"I thought you two were over." The chick's friend said.

"Girl please. We'll never be over."

"Excuse me." I said and tossed my paper towel in the trash. Khloe was still washing her hands and staring at the bitch, who was watching her.

"Can I help you?" Khloe asked with an attitude. She may be self-conscious and won't get in her mom's ass but she's far from a punk.

"I was wondering why two fat bitches were in a club that catered to ballers and wealthy niggas. I know you're not tryna catch a man." K smirked, dried her hands and moved closer.

"If you're asking, it must mean you're worried. Have no fear boo. Risky or whoever the man is you speak of, is not in my view." K winked and headed to the door where I was.

"Bitch, I know you didn't fuck my man."

"Ima let you call me a bitch this one time because I'm far from home and I don't wanna go to jail. But let's be clear. Khloe stood in her face, while the other woman pretended to be on the phone. *What a punk?*

"One... I don't know who your man is. Your loud ass mentioned him when you stepped in. And two... how the fuck you in here poppin shit with the tag hanging out your shirt. When a woman does that, it usually means the outfit is going back because she really can't afford it." K moved in her face.

"Before you attack any woman because of how she looks, check yourself out." She took her index finger and flipped it on the woman's top lip and nose.

"Clean it up, coke whore." The bitch ran to the mirror, while her friend looked at us walk out.

"It's always someone." I told her and ran into a hard body. My instincts kicked in and I pushed the person back.

"Awwwww, HELL NO!" I shouted when I noticed who it was. I didn't get a chance to run, speed walk or anything before this nigga pushed and pinned me against the wall.

"What the hell?" Khloe yelled and some dude held her back. *This nigga about to kill me.*

Waleed

I saw her as soon as she stepped off the elevator. How the fuck was she able to afford a room in this hotel? A room on the first floor alone, cost fifteen hundred. Then, I peeped her expensive ass luggage at the airport and now these clothes and shoes she had on, were a pretty penny. Hell, I didn't even know Louboutin made shoes to fit thick chicks. She's not fat but definitely big boned and her ass was nice and fat. I could see myself digging in her guts and watching it jiggle.

Shorty wasn't ugly and I could tell she was of Spanish descent by her accent and skin color. The long black hair gave it away too. Her mouth was reckless as fuck, but I'm gonna make her eat those words she spoke at the airport.

****

When we got to the club, I wanted a certain section because it had a stripper pole in it. We frequented here a lot and that spot allowed us, our own private strippers. The owner told us one of his friends' daughters came to town and he gave it to her. I wasn't mad because he always catered to us but I still wanted to know who had my spot. I didn't know who it was until I saw the same guys who walked out the hotel behind this chick standing there. I turned around and peeped her and the same chick coming out the bathroom.

"What was all that shit you were talking at the airport?" I stared in her face and she had a sneaky grin on it.

"I didn't stutter and why you sweating me?" She attempted to push me away and I grabbed both of her hands.

"I can't hear you." I let her hands go and used mine to pinch both of her nipples. She didn't have a dick so this is as close as I could get to returning the favor.

"Ssssss." I had to grin at her nasty ass. She was loving this.

"Let me find out you're a freak."

"You should've known when I grabbed this." She let her hand go in my jeans. I guess she thought I'd move it but I let her get free feels.

"You like that?" She bit down on her lip and my shit bricked up. I've never been with a BBW type chick and yet,

54

she was turning me on. I wonder if all the stories were true about them having the best pussy ever.

"What's up then?" I asked and before she could respond, I saw a hand come around my face and connect to hers. I turned and jumped in front of her.

"What you doing with my man?" Dora's stupid ass yelled out. How the hell she yelling that and her ass is with Lamar?

"This dirty bitch is your girl?" I busted out laughing because Dora did look dirty. I don't know if it was her skin color, the clothes or what but she did look as if she belonged on the street.

"Really Waleed? You were in my bed two days ago and.-"

"Correction. You were sucking my dick in your bed but I wasn't laying in it. There's a difference."

"Why you with this fat bitch anyway?" Once she said that, shorty slid from behind me and started giving her the business. Outta nowhere, I noticed three big dudes blocking the view so no one could see. Were they really letting her get shit off? I broke them up and the Spanish chick didn't have a mark on her but Dora, was a different story.

"Risky, what's this?" I looked up and my boy was blocking an angry chick from whooping Ronny's ass.

"Y'all need to go." He told her but she didn't listen.

"Risky, I know you're not entertaining this big bitch." He stepped out the way and this chick beat the brakes off Veronica. I mean, banged her head in the wall and kneed her a few times in the chest and stomach. Who the bell taught them how to fight?

"Aight. That's enough." My boy finally pulled the chick off Veronica who now looked half dead. Both of the women, stepped over them and went to their VIP area. We looked at each other and were laughing so hard we had to hold hour stomachs. Dora and Ronny, were always in some shit and we usually pulled them outta it but not today.

"What the hell y'all doing here?" I asked Dora who was helping Ronny up.

"It's spring break. We always come with y'all." I sucked my teeth. I messed with Dora off and on for about the same amount of time Risky and Ronny were together. The difference is, I didn't claim her, nor did anyone ever see us out. I'm sure Lamar wouldn't be too happy she was here. He wasn't really my boy so him sleeping with her made me no never mind.

"I'm out yo. They killed my vibe." Risky went to walk off and I noticed the two chicks in VIP looking down mad as hell. I nodded my head and the one I was standing with gave me the finger as usual. I must admit, she intrigued me. Most of the chicks in our area would either bow down to Dora or say talking to me wasn't worth the drama.

"Give me a sec." He told me to meet him at the car. I walked up the steps and the guys stopped me.

"What?" She had her arms folded.

"Get yo ass over here." The smirk on her face only verified she was down for the cause. The guys moved out the way and she took one step down.

"What's your room number?" I asked to see if she'd give it to me.

"For?"

"What you think?" I licked my lips.

"I'm not that type of chick." She tried to walk away and I snatched her arm.

"Don't play fucking games with me. I'm too old for that and so are you."

"How bout you give me your room number and key? Maybe I'll surprise you." She had me thinking.

"Nah. I don't know what type of chick you are." She took another step down.

"Boo you don't have anything I want besides this." She grabbed my shit again.

"Anything you buy, I can buy myself. And since we don't know each other there's no need to spend any extra time together than necessary."

"That's what the fuck I'm talking about. So what's up?"

"Room number and key?" She put her hand out and like the horny nigga I am, handed it over. She winked and put the key in her pocket. I shook my head, walked down the steps and was on my way out when Risky pulled my arm. Evidently, he wasn't ready to go and shit I'm down to watch ass jiggle. The whole time shorty and I, eye fucked the hell outta one another. A few times she pretended to dance on the pole and my dick was semi hard. Like I said before, I've never been with a chick her size but I'm down to try it out that's for sure.

****

Risky and I ended up leaving not too long after them and came to the hotel. I had to tell the receptionist I lost my key so she'd give me a new one because I gave it to the chick. I hopped in the shower and fell asleep, only for her to wake me up with some head and she was doing a decent job. It's sad, I didn't even know her name.

"Damn ma. You doing your thing." I lifted myself on my elbows and watched shorty swallow me whole. Well, I was watching someone because it was dark in here.

"Yo! What the fuck?" I pushed Dora's head back and stood up. I had no idea it was her at first until she did her signature move. As of lately, the bitch stayed tryna lick my asshole, which is why I never let her suck my dick after the last time.

"How you get in here?" I shut the light on and one of her eyes were black and she had a busted lip.

"And how you even attempting to put your mouth on my shit with an open sore?"

"Waleed."

"Don't Waleed me bitch. It's still open and has dried up blood on it. Oh hell no." I grabbed my keys, phone and went to the door.

"Where you going?"

"To the fucking ER. One... you hit me off with no condom and you know I don't play that shit. And two... you in here looking like Rhonda Roussey after she got her ass beat, tryna fuck. Yo, can you even see out that eye?" She snatched her things up and walked over to me.

"Why you treating me like this?"

"Have you seen your face?"

"It's not that bad." I opened the camera on my phone and snapped.

"What you doing?"

"Showing you what your face looks like." I turned it to her and she pushed it away.

"So you do know what you look like?" I pushed her in the hallway and closed the door.

"Hmph. A minute man I see." I looked down and shorty from the club was sitting on the ground. What the hell is going on?

"What you doing out here?" She rolled on her knees and I could see how fat that ass was and grabbed myself. She stood and wiped her pajama pants off.

"Well. Me and my girl came back here after the club." Dora had the nerve to roll her eyes as shorty spoke. She got some nerve getting mad when she snuck in my damn room.

"Per our conversation, I cleaned myself up, and made my way to your floor, only to find this got damn stalker tryna break in." I looked at Dora who gave her a weak smile.

"Anyway, she informed me of all the fat bitches you called me and said you wouldn't waste your time with someone like me." I was getting angrier by the second. My dick never discriminated against pussy. I was equal opportunity like a motherfucker.

"Instead of coming in, I handed her the key and told her to have at it. That literally was seven minutes ago." She looked at her phone.

"Which is why I said you were a minute man."

"Yo hold on." She put her hand up. I tried to tell her the bitch was lying but she wasn't tryna hear it.

"I'm good Waleed." She shoulder checked the shit outta Dora and her entire body hit the wall. I saw all that ass walking away and yoked Dora up.

"I don't care if you see a woman standing at my door with one leg, no nails, teeth missing and a smelly pussy. You better keep it moving. Do I make myself clear?" At first, she didn't answer but after I yelled in her face, she knew I wasn't playing and said yes. I heard the elevator door bing and tried to catch it before it closed. *Damn!* I had no idea what her name was, or the floor she had a room on. If its meant for me to see her again, I will.

I took my ass to the local urgent care and explained

how a chick with a cold sore sucked me off while I was drunk.

After the lady laughed, she gave me a shot of penicillin and

said it was in case she fucked me and I wasn't aware. She

could laugh all she wants, as long as my ass had a shot, I'm

good. I drove back to the hotel and took my ass to my room

mad as hell, I didn't get to sample that pussy from the chick. I

made sure the door was locked and had that extra lock on it.

I'll be damned if the bitch comes back and tries again.

Risky

"What Veronica?" I shouted in my phone after she called for the hundredth time. I just got in my room and was tired as hell.

"Can I come to your room? We need to talk."

"Bet." I gave her the room information and waited for her to arrive.

I brushed my teeth and lit a black and mild because she was about to pull me outta character. This will be the first time speaking to her after hearing what she did to Raina or had her doing. I tried a few times to get at her but my mom begged me not to.

When I heard a knock at the door, I blew my breath and opened it. She entered and I was about to close it when the chick from the club Waleed was talking to, walked by. I doubt she noticed me but I paid attention to which door she stopped at. I wanted to speak to her friend and I couldn't do it at the club or right now. I'm gonna make it my business to hit her up afterwards.

"What Veronica?" I felt her come behind me in the small kitchen and wrap her arms around my waist.

"I miss you." She placed a kiss on the middle of my back. I still loved and missed her too but I would never be with a woman who made my daughter think her weight is an issue. Not only that, she must've forgotten about the video and the fact she cheated. I turned around and that's when I realized she had a black eye and the side of her face was swollen.

"What you miss Ronny?" She allowed her finger to slide down my chest and to my stomach. I stopped her before she could get any further and bent her wrist backwards.

"What are you doing?"

"Have you been telling Raina she's fat?" I now had her arm twisted behind her back and her face against the wall.

"No. I would never."

"Did you teach her how to be bulimic or had her sticking fingers down her throat?" She gave me a weird look and I couldn't tell if she were lying but it didn't matter. Whatever my daughter said to my mother regarding the issue, is what I believe.

"I love Raina like she's my own."

"Is that right?"

"Yes Risky. I would never hurt her."

"Since lies roll right off your tongue, roll the fuck up outta here." I opened the door and tossed her out.

"Stay away from my daughter and don't make me repeat myself." I slammed the door in her face, slid on my slippers and grabbed my keys and phone. I waited a few minutes to make sure Ronny left, opened the door and walked to the door I saw the chick going in earlier. I knocked and waited for someone to answer. When the door opened, the woman smirked and yelled out for someone named Khloe. I guess she knew I wasn't there for her.

"You can come in." I stepped in and she left me standing there. I heard one door open and another one close.

"What Luna?" She shouted and walked out in a satin like pajama shirt that stopped at her knees. Once she saw me, she became embarrassed and closed the robe.

"Ummmm. What are you doing here?" I walked closer to her and her breathing increased. It appears that a nigga like me, already had her panties wet.

"Damn, you smell good."

"Thanks, but what are..." I let my hand go behind her head, tilted it back and my tongue did the rest. I pushed her against the wall, untied the robe and both of my hands cupped her ass cheeks. I'm not sure what made me do it, but I didn't want it to end.

"Mmmmmm. We have to stop." She pushed me away but only a little.

"Yea we do." We stared at one another and no words were spoken as I followed her in the room and closed the door. She turned the lock, removed the shirt and my dick grew. Shorty had no stomach, her legs and arms were big, her titties were perky and that ass was perfect.

"Damn you sexy." She blushed and tried to cover her smile.

"We don't know each other and I have no expectations after tonight. Just give me something to remember you by."

She said and sat on the bed with her legs open. Who knew she'd be on some one-night stand shit? I ain't the one to complain. If this is what she wants, I'm giving it to her. Her index finger circled her pearl and the other hand caressed her breasts.

"Let me see you cum ma." I leaned on the dresser and watched as her clit began to grow in a matter of seconds. It was sexy as fuck and I found myself stroking my man. After a few minutes, we both came at the same time. Me, in my hand and her on the bed. I went in the connected bathroom, washed my hands and came out to see her at it again. I allowed my shorts and boxers to hit the floor and was just about to handle my business when we heard yelling.

"Shit." She shouted and threw her robe on. I grabbed her arm and told her to put some clothes on and I'll check it out. I opened the door slowly and crept in the other room.

"Get your stupid ass outta here nigga. Go be with the bitch you talked shit about me too." The Luna chick was cursing Waleed out. Now me knowing the type of nigga he is, felt this was about to escalate. Yes, he's a comedian but he's

68

also a dangerous nigga who when pushed too far, won't have mercy on you.

"I got your stupid. Check this bitch."

"Whoaaaaaa." Khloe said and came towards him.

"Nah ma. Get back." She smiled and I winked at the same time I was pushing Waleed out the door.

"Fuck you and that bitch." Luna was poppin mad shit and he was becoming angrier.

"Let's go bro. It ain't worth it."

CLICK! I heard and turned around to see Luna holding a gun.

"Wrong move bitch." And just that fast, shit went left. Waleed pulled his piece out and I heard the bullet whisked past my ear. Luna let off and Khloe hit the floor.

"FUCK!" I ran over to her and saw blood coming out her shoulder.

"Look what the fuck you two idiots did."

"Oh my God K. Are you ok?" Luna had tears coming down her face. I looked at Waleed.

"I'm not tryna be funny but I can't help you lift her." I heard another noise and Luna was shooting at him again. I couldn't believe this shit. I ran in the bathroom to grab a towel and looked in her room for a belt. Once I found one, I went in the living room to find Waleed and Luna holding a gun at each other's head.

"Yo, we gotta get her to a hospital." Luna picked her phone up and not even five minutes later, a doctor came rushing in and moved me out the way. The three guys from the club came barging in and started fighting with Waleed. After helping the doctor get Khloe in the other room, I came out, picked his gun up and let off in the ceiling. Thank goodness this was the highest floor; otherwise somebody would've been shot.

"Calm y'all asses down. He can't concentrate. Tha fuck is you two thinking?" Waleed got another hit off on one of the guys and knocked him out.

"Get out!" Luna opened the door.

"Not until my boy leaves."

"He can go too." I walked up on her.

70

"Look shorty. I don't give two fucks who you are or what type of shit you into but what you won't do, is play tough with me. I'll snap your fucking neck and step over you as if nothing happened." This is the first time I saw fear on her face. It could because I was calm when I said it or the fact my arm was around her throat.

"Do I make myself clear?" She nodded and let me know she understood

"Ima let you go and I promise if you try any funny shit, I'll tell him to kill you." I pointed to my boy who was twirling the gun on his thumb.

"Why are you still here? You don't even know her like that?" She was rubbing her neck and had some nerve questioning me after the shit her and my boy were doing.

"And?"

"And you could be in your own room."

"I came to see if she was ok from the club drama. Then we started talking, you two were acting like fools and she got shot. What type of nigga am I, if I leave her and you two go at it again? Y'all dumb as hell for this." I wasn't gonna tell her

71

what we were really doing. That's her friend. If she wanted her to know she could tell her.

I went in the back where the doctor had Khloe laying. I was happy as hell she threw some leggings and a T-shirt on before she came out the room. Otherwise she would've given everyone a show. Don't ask me why it mattered when I barely knew her.

"Ok. All finished." The doctor said and placed a big piece of gauze over her.

"How is she?"

"It's a flesh wound but she did hit her head pretty hard. It's most likely a concussion and since there's a knot forming, I'm not too concerned. What I will say is, keep those people away from her." I laughed.

"Yea I know." He shook my hand and walked out. I looked around the room and blood was on her sheets and the comforter. I yelled out for Luna to call downstairs for a new set.

I rolled Khloe over gently to remove the sheets and she stirred a little but didn't get up. Once Luna came in with the

72

stuff, she helped me fix the sheets and laid a towel under Khloe's arm to make sure no leftover blood was on the sheet. She claims her friend is very neat and will have a fit if she woke up like that.

"Soooooo, can you take your friend outta here?" Luna questioned and pointed to Waleed who still had an evil look on his face.

"I'm not going nowhere until I feel like it." This nigga was fucking with her.

"Ughhhhhh!" She stormed out the room and his dumb ass smacked her hard as hell on the ass. I thought she'd punch him or something but she kept it moving. You could hear the door slam and he fell out laughing. I took one last look at Khloe and pushed him out the room. He went straight to the other bedroom and kicked the door in. I ran behind him and he had shorty by her hair.

"I'm gonna sample that pussy one of these days." He crashed his lips on hers and slammed her on the bed.

"Yo, I'm out. You doing dumb shit." I heard a loud thump and he was picking the remote up of the floor. She must've tossed it at him on the way out.

"Let's go." He threw it back in the room and came out behind me.

"What the fuck yo?" I opened the room to my door and this dumb bitch was playing with her pussy on my couch. How the hell did she even get in here?

"I miss you Risky." She moaned out with her eyes closed.

"He don't miss your ass." She pulled her fingers out and tried to cover herself. That's what she gets for sneaking in here.

"I'll see you in the morning." I closed the door and left her sitting there. I didn't feel like arguing and hopped in the shower.

"Is that blood?" She pointed to my basketball shorts on the ground.

"How did you get in here?"

"I told the lady at the front we were married and I locked myself out the room."

I sucked my teeth. When she stepped in, I didn't even bother to stop her.

"I know you miss me too baby." She stroked my man to life, kneeled down and went to work on me. I'm not even going to lie. When I stared down at her like I always do, Khloe was the one down there doing it. I guess when you're imagining someone else, it feels ten times better because I damn sure came harder than normal. I don't know what it is about Khloe or why I even showed up at her door, but I had to learn more about her.

Once Ronny finished sucking me off, I went in the bedroom, closed the door, locked it and went to sleep. I needed a nut after seeing Khloe handle herself but the other two fools messed it up.

I hope Ronny knows just because she hit me off, that nothing's changed. My daughter will always be my priority and the shit she had Raina doing is an automatic cut off. I would kill her but I promised my mom, she wouldn't die by my hands. My mother knew a lot about some of the things I've done in the streets. Even though I deny them to her, she ain't stupid. At least, with Ronny out the picture, she can't fuck with my daughter any longer but if she does, then my mom will have to understand.

Khloe

I woke up this morning with a stiff upper body and a humongous headache. I looked at my arm and couldn't remember what the hell happened. I do know that sexy ass man Risky was here. I let him watch me play with myself and I watched him to the same. We were about to get it in and Luna started yelling and... Oh my God! I heard a gun go off and... I glanced at my arm again and that's when I noticed a sling and some pills next to the bed. Did I get shot and if so, who did it? It had to be that crazy ass man Risky was with.

I sat up and let my legs slide off the bed. It was a struggle tryna stand but I did it and went in the bathroom. I looked on the sink and there was a note that read, *I enjoyed watching you and definitely wanna spend some more time with you. Here's my number. Call me when you get up.* I put the letter against my chest and smiled. I thought it would be a one-night stand but maybe not. I mean, we didn't actually have sex so it wouldn't be considered one, would it? I wouldn't care if he wanted to meet up again and have one, because he was fine as hell.

He was at least six foot four or five, with the most beautiful hazel eyes. He was a tad bit on the skinny side but I could still see the muscles coming out the shirt. His tongue was long and thick and the thought of him sliding it between my pink folds had me fantasizing. Then the way his dick hung made me nervous. Its been a minute since I had some and here I was about to hop on his long and thick pole. My pussy would've probably been extra sore today.

KNOCK! KNOCK! I heard and rushed to brush my teeth the best I could with the use of one arm. I didn't know if it were the guy and wasn't about to get caught slipping with bad breath.

"We have to go." I walked in the room and noticed Luna packing my bag. She seemed nervous and it scared me.

"What happened last night Luna?" She proceeded to give me the highlights of her and dude fighting, and then how they shot at one another and I was hit with the stray. She was hysterical crying and apologizing. I know she didn't mean to hit me but at the same time, they were both being careless as fuck.

"I hear what you saying but it doesn't explain why we're leaving." She stood with her arms folded as I grabbed a towel to take a bath, since I couldn't shower.

"He came in the room, yanked me up by the hair and told me he was sampling my pussy. Threw his tongue down my throat and tossed me on the bed." I had to look and see if she were serious and when I noticed she was, I busted out laughing.

"Bitch, that's not funny. I threw the remote and hit him in the back. Do you know he tossed it back and caught me in the forehead? Look." She lifted her hair and I saw the knot.

"Luna, you and him are a match made in heaven."

"I don't even know him." She sucked her teeth and waved me off.

"Hurry up so we can go."

"I'm not ready to leave."

"Khloe, do you want him to kill your best friend?" She was in front of me.

"You're being dramatic. Can you start the water?" She leaned over and did it for me but not without begging me to leave with her. After watching her pout, I agreed. I mean dude did give me his number so even though I can't get to know him now, I can later.

After getting out the tub and getting all of our things together, she called the bodyguards in. They each looked like they were in a brawl. One had a black eye, one had a sling on his arm and one walked with a limp. What the hell went on in here while I was out? I glanced at Luna and she shrugged her shoulders but I know better. Whatever went down had to do with her. Shit, its what they're here for. On our way out, a door opened and both of us stopped.

"I'm going to change Risky. I'll be back." She said and looked over at us. I knew she was being smart.

"Looks like you had a rough night." She pointed to my arm. I could hurt her feelings and tell her it didn't matter if she came from inside because he was obviously with me first or left her to come see me but I'll pass. If she's coming out his room, why even waste my breath?

"Bitch, you need something?" Luna stood in her face and the chick put her hands up in surrender.

"All I need is to wash this cum off and pray he got me pregnant."

"Pathetic." I was loud enough for her to hear.

"Pathetic? Nope." She put her index finger on her chin.

"Smart? Yes." She came over to me.

"Smart enough to trap and keep him away from any bitch who tries to destroy what we built over the last four years." She backed away.

"Oh, but you can do me a favor and figure out a way to keep his fat ass daughter out the picture." My mouth dropped and so did Luna's.

"What?" She shrugged her shoulders.

"She's a pain in the ass. All she does is eat and its not a good look on my future baby daddy, slash husband."

"Are you serious?" I asked because a grown woman couldn't be speaking this ill of a child.

"As a heart attack boo. She's a reflection of him and he won't be made a fool of because his daughter wants to be the size of a giant marshmallow. Looks like you two will have a lot in common." I tried to go after her but Luna stopped me.

The bitch ran down the stairway and as bad as I wanted to knock on his door and inform him of her childish antics, I kept it moving. If he's been with her that long, he'll have to figure shit out on his own.

I pulled the small note out my pocket with his number on it and tossed it in the trash can by the elevator. I don't need those type of problems in my life. Its for the best anyway. Neither of us exchanged any info and I have no idea where he's from. As the saying goes, you can't miss what you never had.

****

"How are you sweetie?" My dad asked when he stopped by. I hadn't seen him since I returned from vacation and that was a couple of weeks ago. Plus, he's been working so much I barely speak to him.

"I'm good." I moved around the kitchen with ease now that I removed the sling. After a few days, I took that shit off.

The doctor said I healed up nicely and still wanted me to wear it but I was over it.

"You know that chile is crazy. What was she doing playing with her gun anyway?"

"We were bored." I shrugged and went along with the original story I gave him, which was; Luna and I were in the room, she was bored and played with the gun. Unfortunately, it went off and caught me in the shoulder. That's my story and I'm sticking with it.

"Come sit. I need to talk to you." I saw the uneasiness in his face, dropped the fork I used to mix my chicken stir fry and took a seat next to him. He ran his hand down my face and smiled.

"This is going to come as a shock but it's been a long time in the making." I felt that nervousness in my stomach. He told me to relax because no one was hurt. He knew of my condition and made sure not to ever stress me out.

"I'm leaving your mom." I smiled and so did he. We both knew he was unhappy.

"She's not the woman I married."

"I know. She's not exactly mother material either." He nodded.

"I'm sorry for the way she treated you all these years. The sad part is, I can't even tell you why she did it." He had a stressful look on his face.

"Is she my real mother?" I asked because I've read in books how a woman who raised another woman's child, treated her like shit. The signs pointed in that direction too. He chuckled and rested his head on the back of the seat.

"Unfortunately, she is. I held her hand and watched her push you out."

"Dammit!" I was hoping he said no.

"Is she really that bad?" He asked and I looked at him.

"You tell me dad. You're the one leaving her."

"Yea, she is but look. I'm going to see a house today. Do you wanna come with me?"

"Really? Daddy, you could've stayed here with me."

"She's here too much and I need some peace and quiet. Hell, it's one of the reasons I'm leaving. Well that, and her putting us in extreme debt." I covered my mouth.

"Why didn't you tell me? Daddy, you know I would've helped." He grabbed both sides of my face and looked in my eyes.

"No matter how old you are, you're still my child and I'm supposed to take care of you, not the other way around. I am so proud of you Khloe and even though I may not say it enough, just know that I am and no matter what, you will always be number one in my life."

"Same here dad." I hugged him and jumped up to check on my food, I had to put on low.

"How are you buying a new house if you're in debt?" I yelled from the kitchen and he came in.

"Why you think I've been working so much?" I turned around. My dad was literally working seven days a week and has been for a few years. I never knew why but now I do.

"I've paid every credit card and loan she's ever put in both of our names. Even the cars are on their last few monthly payments. Baby, I am finally debt free and before she realizes it and does it again, I'm leaving. This way with a divorce, she can only put things in her own name."

"That's very smart dad."

"I don't want her to go into debt but I can't stress myself anymore over it because its only gonna drive me in an early grave and I still haven't met my grandkids."

"Not today daddy." He couldn't wait for me to have children but I kept telling him, ain't no man gonna have kids with a fat girl. I think he's in denial about how big I really am and secretly hopes a man sweeps me off my feet. The only man, I wanted to have a kid with, obviously chose another woman to birth his mini me's.

After putting some clothes on and eating lunch with my dad, we headed over to the spot the house was located. The area was nice and there had to be an expensive car or truck in each of the driveways.

He parked in front of a huge blue house. I asked how many bedrooms and he said four. One for him, one for me and Luna because he knew if I stayed over, she would be with me and one for his grandkid. I had to laugh at that.

I opened the door and both of us walked around the yard and into the back. There was a small in ground pool and a few benches. You could see the glass doors that led to the kitchen. I peeked in and stared in amazement. From the outside looking in, there were stainless steel appliances and the floor appeared to be brand new. I asked him how much was the asking price and when the answer came out, it wasn't from him. I turned around and stared into the eyes of the man, I assumed I left in Florida. What the hell is he doing here in Jersey?

Risky

PHEW! PHEW! PHEW! PHEW!

I watched all four bodies take their last breath, as the bullets from my gun went through their foreheads.

"You know the drill." I told the guys who were there to clean the mess up. I'd have them present during the killings and then make them drop the person or person(s) off somewhere and set up a fake crime scene. That way it'll never trace back to any of us. Afterwards, I'd go home like nothing happened, chill with my daughter and wait for the call from the family at the hospital, asking me to pick the body up to do the service. Yea, I'm a grimy nigga but fuck it. If the niggas don't pay their debt while they're still alive, at least I'll collect some of it, in their death.

"Hurry up. I need to show this house so I can get it off my hands." I walked to the back of the warehouse, removed the gloves from my hand and tossed them and the gun down the incinerator. Like I said, always cover your tracks and no one can place you at the scene.

"Bro, you couldn't wait for me?" Waleed shouted coming in the door. The killings were for him and he said he'd be here a half hour ago and he's just walking in. He was late to everything.

"You took too long and I told you, I had shit to do."

"What the fuck ever. Look at this shit." He pulled me to the side and showed me a video off one of the cameras he had placed in his spots. It showed Lamar and Dora sneaking in and rummaging through the place.

"What the hell they looking for?"

"Hell if I know. And before you ask, I ain't never brought that bitch out the house. I damn sure wouldn't show her this." I may not be in the drug life anymore but Waleed knew what I would say regarding that, which is why he said it first.

"Is anything missing?"

"Nah. I watched the entire thing and whatever they wanted, it wasn't there."

"Since when Lamar need to steal?"

"This has Dora's dumb ass written all over it but then again, who knows." He closed the app and asked if I ever heard from the chicks in Florida.

I thought about tryna find her but decided against it. I left my phone number and told her to contact me. If she didn't, it's safe to assume I'm not what she wanted and I'm fine with that. Especially; with annoying ass Ronny still around. I don't know what I was thinking letting her in my room. I guess being horny had a way of getting me in trouble.

"What's up with Ronny? I thought you weren't fucking with her no more after what ma dukes told you she said about my niece. Shit, had you not loved her at one point I would've put a bullet in her already." I felt the same way, which is why she is no longer allowed around Raina and shockingly my daughter never asked about her again, after I told her we broke up. I wonder if she were happy.

"To be honest, I'm only fucking her and it'll stay that way until I find someone else." I'm not the type of dude to go around slinging dick and since I'm familiar with her, it is, what it is. Don't get it twisted tho. I don't stay the night, I'm no longer funding her lifestyle, can't even tell you where she's staying and the two vehicles I got her; re poed those. As far as money, she gets nothing from me. Ronny does complain and whine about being broke and the minute I mention her getting a job, she shuts the fuck up. When I said she was there to satisfy my sexual needs only, that's what I meant. It may not be right but its my business.

"Aight yo. I'm on my way to show the house. What you about to do?"

"I may as well come with you since you took away my daily dose of killing." I had to laugh at his silly ass. Waleed had jokes for days and as I mentioned before, when he's serious, another side of him shows and no one wants to be a part of that.

****

We parked behind a brand new GLS Mercedes truck and noticed no one was in it. I looked around the house and saw two figures going towards the back. It had to be the individuals who were looking to purchase. I checked myself over to make sure no blood splattered off and into my clothes.

91

"Bro. Not right now." I snatched the blunt out his hand and put it in my pocket. At least, it would keep him from lighting up on the front porch. He went to the mailbox and grabbed the mail while I headed to the rear. I heard a woman asking someone how much. Once I answered and she turned around, a smile graced my face.

"Hello. My name is Ryan Wells and you must be Mr. Banks." I shook his hand and saw Khloe put her head down.

"I am. Do you mind if we look inside?"

"Not at all." I stepped out the way and allowed the two of them to walk ahead of me. I heard Khloe gasp as she opened the door. I had showroom furniture here for any potential buyers. It helps sell the place and right now I think it's doing the job. We started to tour the place and Waleed was already inside watching television.

"Why is he here?" Khloe asked and he turned around.

"Oh shit yo. Long time no see. Where your sexy friend at. She owes me."

"Owes you?" She folded her arms and I took her dad in the kitchen.

"Hell Yea. She promised to take a ride on the Waleed train and a nigga still waiting."

"I can't with you." I could still hear them from the kitchen. She came back in to where we were, ran her hand across the counter space and admired the decor. Shorty, had an eye for nice things. Everything in this bitch was top of the line from the floors to the shower stalls. Ronny was spoiled as hell by me.

"Oooh, I can't wait to see the bedrooms." She was excited as hell. I watched her dad go up the steps and followed directly behind her. My hands couldn't hold out any longer and squeezed both of her cheeks when she reached the top of the steps. She swatted my hand away and her dad turned around.

"I'm guessing that you two know one another." Her entire face turned red.

"We met on vacation dad. Look how big this room is." Her dad smiled and walked out to look in the others. I closed the door, locked it and went to her in the master bathroom.

"Oh shit. You scared me." She jumped when I stood behind her.

"Why didn't you call?" I let my hands roam under her shirt and lifted it over her head.

"Sit up here." She placed herself on top of the sink and I stood in between her legs. I stared at her and now that no liquor is in my system, I could see how pretty she really is. The mole on top of her lip made her smile even better.

"I didn't think you wanted me to, since I saw the same chick I beat up leaving the room."

"You can't believe everything you see." I unsnapped her bra and watched her titties spill out. They were big and juicy.

"We can't do this here..." is what she said but didn't stop me from sucking on them.

"I want you Khloe but you're right. This isn't a good place. Can I stop by your house later?"

"Only if you let me do this."

"Do what?" She unbuckled my jeans and made them and my boxers hit the floor.

"Make you cum in my hand."

"You drive a hard bargain but... Shittt ma." She was stroking me gently and rough at the same time. I couldn't even explain the feeling she was giving me. My eyes closed, my body stiffened up and I felt her lips on my neck.

"I can't wait to feel you inside me. Ryan, are you gonna give me what I want?" She whispered and my dick threw up in her hand like she asked. I thought that was good but when she licked it off her hand, I knew she was a freak and we were about to turn each other out.

"You taste good baby. Keep drinking water." She moved me back and leaned over to wash her hands.

"If your pops weren't here, I'd pull these fucking pants off and stick my dick in you."

"These are thick walls, right?" She asked with a devious smirk on her face.

"Yea."

"Then do you." I wasted no time unbuttoning her pants from behind. She had on no panties and her ass busted out. My man was super hard and rushing me to enter. I spread those cheeks and saw her juices were dripping. I had no business about to enter this woman I knew nothing about without a condom, but my dick was too hard for me to stop now. It took me a minute to get in, due to how tight she was. However, the feeling was outta this world.

"AHHHHHH FUCCCCCKKKKK!" She yelled and gripped the sink when I entered. We both stared at one another in the mirror as we let our bodies become in sync.

"Damn, I knew this pussy would be good." Her juices were sliding down my leg like someone spilled juice on me. Once she started twerking on me, I asked her to bend over and touch those ankles.

KNOCK! KNOCK! KNOCK! We heard and she jumped. I knew it was stupid ass Waleed by the way he knocked but she wasn't tryna hear it and made me stop.

"Oh my God. I can't believe we just... But it was feeling so good." She wiped herself with some tissues, pulled her pants up and I did the same.

"I'm still coming by later. What's your address?" I held her in the corner. This time she wasn't getting away. She gave me the address, kissed me and ran to open the door.

"I'll see you later."

"What the fuck were y'all doing?" Waleed was grinning. Her hair was a tad bit messed up and you could see how outta breath she was.

"He was fucking me until you knocked. Blocking ass nigga." She pushed him to the side and we both started laughing.

"Yo, I have to know." I washed my hands and looked at the hickey she left on my neck. I didn't mind because it was in the heat of the moment and I'm not with anyone.

"What?"

"Neither one of us ever had a big girl. Was it as good as niggas say?"

"What the hell you talking about?"

"Man, how many times these niggas told us they fucked a fat chick and the pussy was bomb?" I thought about what he said and a lot of dudes definitely said that.

"Man, I'm only telling you." I dried my hands on one of the towels hanging.

"Bro, I know that. I wouldn't dare ask you in front of anyone else. So tell me." I think he was interested because of her friend. Waleed wanted her bad and it's only because she's a challenge. His rude ass had bitches throwing the pussy at him.

"For those few minutes I felt inside, I'd have to say she has the best pussy I've felt thus far."

"I FUCKING KNEW IT!"

"There's only one problem." We were walking down the steps

"And what's that?" I stared at Khloe and her dad talking on the front porch.

"I would never make her my girl."

"Say what now?" He snatched me by the shoulder and made me look at him.

"She's not the woman I can see myself having a future with."

"Please tell me it's not because of her weight." Waleed dated any woman. Big, small, ugly or whatever. As long as she was good to him, he didn't care. Me on the other hand. I had an image to protect and no matter how good the pussy is, I'm not messing it up for anyone.

"I'm sure she's a good woman but not for me."

"I'm gonna say this and leave it alone." He helped me turn the lights off.

"If you don't see a future with her, maybe you should leave her alone."

"Why would I do that? I just told you she has fire between those big ass thighs." I went to grab the door handle.

"And you also said you don't want a woman her size and from the way she seemed smitten by you, I can tell she's gonna fall hard. Why even put her through it?" He opened the door and asked me to unlock the car. I stood there staring and thinking about what he said.

"Son, I'll take it." Her dad said snapping me out my thoughts.

"That's great. I'll have the contract drawn up and sent. Khloe, I'll see you later." I shook her dads hand and winked at her. I don't care what Waleed said. I'm getting that pussy again and I'll leave her alone before she falls.

Khloe

"Took you long enough." I said to Risky, Ryan or whatever his name is, when he knocked on the door.

I bit my lip as I surveyed his outfit. The gray sweats only showed me exactly what I was waiting for. I still couldn't believe the two of us had a damn quickie in the house. It felt good as hell tho.

After I left seeing the house with my dad, I dropped him off and came home to straighten up. I told Luna what happened and she cursed me out for talking to him. She claimed that now if we start sleeping together, his crazy ass friend is gonna find her. She was being extra dramatic, which is why I didn't tell her he asked about her and said she owes him. I'd have to hear a whole sob story on that too. I have no idea why she's acting that way, knowing damn well she wants him. I mean, its all she talked about on the way back.

"Shut that shit up and strip." He made sure the locks were on the door, followed me up the steps and I did what he asked. My nightgown hit the floor but my heels were still on. I wasn't a bad bitch at all and I'm still self-conscious about my body but he had a way to make me forget about my flaws, dimples and areas of cellulite. Maybe its because a man as fine as him, wanted someone like me. Even if it was just sex, the fact that he's here, says a lot.

I saw him staring at my ass and smirked. It sat up high but it wasn't perfectly round like these social media tricks and skinny women. The only thing I can say I took my pride in, is my stomach and that's because it's flat.

"Your turn." I said when he locked the bedroom door. He did it and grinned when he saw the few toys on my dresser and the sheer curtain that draped from my canopy bed. Hell yea, I'm a freak.

"Mmmm, that looks very tasty." I pointed to his dick and walked over to him.

"Come see." I squatted in front of him and licked the tip slowly. His hands gripped my hair and pulled it back so he could watch. I was about to put a show on for him and stopped to do something else first.

I grabbed the edible massage oil off the bed, squirted a little on my hand and then let it glide all over him. It was weird doing it as he stood but he enjoyed it nonetheless.

"Let me show you what you've been missing." I placed kisses down his body and licked my lips when I was face to face with his prized possession.

"Shittttt girl." And just like that, my mouth was wrapped around his man and he was moaning out my name. I deep throated all of him and even gagged a little to make it more dramatic. He begged me to stop but I couldn't. My hands were twisting and turning as I licked in between his legs and up to his balls. I juggled them in my mouth and spit them out like candy. The sound drove him insane. I was loving every minute of it and by his moans, so was he.

"Cum in my mouth baby. Let me taste all that delicious ass cum you got." His body stiffened, his head went back and I felt him twitching. When his sperm hit my throat, I sucked even harder and he almost fell from how weak his knees were.

"Got damn K." I stood and kissed his stomach, chest and neck again. He was still tryna control his breathing while I

102

was stroking him back to life. I hadn't had dick in a while and the sample he gave me earlier only made my hunger for it, grow.

"My turn." He pushed me on the bed, spread my legs and rubbed his hands together as if he were winning a prize. To be honest, I didn't think he would go down on me and I wouldn't have been upset if he didn't.

"Did anybody ever mention how pretty your pussy is?" He asked and lifted each of my legs on his shoulders.

"You're the first man, I've allowed to see me fully naked in a very long time. So to answer your question; no." It was true. Marcus is the only man I've allowed to see me like this and it took a very long time for it to happen. Now, anytime I slept with a guy, it had to be damn near pitch black in the room. I didn't want them staring at me and get turned off. My insecurities about my body always got the best of me.

"Good. Keep it that way. Nobody needs to see, touch or taste this anymore but me." I was about to respond but him French kissing my clit and inserting two fingers stopped me. I gripped the sheets as the force of the first orgasm began to come down. My body shook and the blood could be felt racing through my veins. At least, I thought I could feel it. That's how good it was feeling. He sucked a tad bit harder and it felt like all my insides escaped.

"Yea ma. That's sexy as fuck." I sat on my elbows and watched him smile as he witnessed my cream coming out. He reached for something and came back over to the bed.

"Thanks. I guessssssssss." I screamed out when he dove back in. I heard a vibrating noise and tried to look up but the next orgasm rushed out like water.

"I wanna try something." I nodded and waited.

"Shittttttttt." I tensed up a little when he pushed the dildo inside.

"Fuck it back K." He was now standing over me. My hips grinded on his hand as he went in and out with the toy. I felt his finger on my clit and the harder it got, the faster he circled.

"Right there. Shit, yes." He stopped.

"Hell no, you not coming off this." He pulled it out and forcefully penetrated me. I dug my nails in his shoulder and once our bodies became in sync, nothing else mattered.

"Is that toy better than me?" His eyes were staring a hole through me as he waited for the answer.

"Nooooooo." I grabbed his neck and our tongues fought against each other. He had my legs over his shoulders, damn near behind my neck, pushed to the side and any other way he could in this missionary position.

"Get on top." I never said a word and switched spots. I took my time because of my weight and didn't wanna crush him or this good ass dick.

"Just like that ma." He squeezed my breasts and bit down on his lip. I rode him this way for a while and turned to do it cowgirl style. He was smacking my ass and once his finger went in my ass, I lost all control and came over and over. It's like I couldn't stop.

"Shit you got some banging ass pussy." He had me on all fours now and literally had me running from the dick. He went in deep and pulled out slow, then had me place one leg on the ground and I promise my intestines has to be twisted from how far it went in. I felt his chest on my back as he continued terrorizing my insides.

"I swear on everything I love, if you fuck another nigga, I'm gonna kill you and him." I smiled to myself but knew he was just talking because of how good it felt. Who does he think he's fooling? A man like him will never, ever be seen with someone my size. Men like him kept the trophy wife on display in front of everyone and fat bitches like me, in the house. I'll be his fake ass girlfriend but he's a damn fool if he thinks I'm not gonna be with anyone else and he will. He had me fucked up on many levels. I went along with him but I also know the truth.

"I'm cumming ma." He drilled faster and harder. I could feel his fingers massaging my nub and within minutes we exploded together.

"Are you on the pill?" He asked after we both came down from the high.

"I haven't been with anyone, so no. But I knew you were coming over and even though we should've used a condom, I got this." I showed him the plan B and he sucked his teeth. Surprised by his reaction, I had to question it.

"Am I missing something?" I picked up a bottle of water that was on my nightstand and twisted the cap, to open it.

"Nah. We good." He started putting his clothes on.

"Look." I wanted him see me taking the pill. I didn't need him saying, I tried to trap him.

"What the fuck ever." He grabbed his things and stormed out the room.

"RYAN!" I shouted and he stopped. I tied the belt on my robe. I knew his street name but felt if we weren't out there, I should call him by his birth name.

"What?" He turned around with his face turned up.

"Did I do something wrong? I don't understand why you're leaving or have an attitude, all of a sudden."

"Why you take that pill?"

"You're confusing me. I mean, how you ask if I'm on the pill and then ask why I took one to make sure you didn't get me pregnant. What's going on?"

"You know what? You're right. I couldn't have a kid with someone like you."

"EXCUSE ME!" I was now storming down the steps and in his direction.

"He means you're too fat and he wouldn't dare plant his seeds in you to make you fatter. What would his friends say?"

"Yo who the fuck are you?" He looked my mom up and down. She shrugged her shoulders and sat on the couch. She always showed up at the wrong times but I couldn't help but assume that what she said is true. Especially, with the comment he made.

"Why you calling her fat? Your ass ain't skinny." Was he defending me to my mother? It's cute but he still didn't respond to her comment.

"Don't you worry about my fat ass. My man like it." She gave him the finger and sipped on whatever she was drinking.

"Is that true Ryan?" He looked at me.

"Yea, Ryan. Is it true? Inquiring minds wanna know."
Now she was fucking with him, but to be honest, I wanted to
know too.

"What?" He asked and stared back at me.

"You said, you couldn't have a baby by someone like
her. What exactly, did you mean?" She smirked like she was
getting a kick out of it and I'm sure she is because she always
got off on me hurting.

"Why you listening to her?" He walked over, kissed me
and left. I locked the door and stared as she shook her head in
disgust.

"When did you get here?" She didn't answer so I left
her sitting there.

"Him kissing you don't mean shit." I stopped walking
up the steps.

"What?"

"Him kissing you don't mean shit because it's in front
of me. See if he'll do that shit in public. I bet he won't." She
flipped through the channels on the TV.

"You think I'm stupid? I know he was here to fuck and guess what? I'm ok with it. I needed some and he supplied it."

"Why did you let him cum in you though?" I leaned against the wall.

"You wanted him to want you, the same way you want him but it'll never be. He's a fine ass nigga and probably one who won't ruin his image for pussy."

"I wasn't thinking."

"Then why buy a pill."

"BECAUSE I WANTED TO FEEL HIM WITHOUT ONE. IS THAT OK? I KNOW THE CONSEQUENCES AND WILL BE AT THE CLINIC TOMORROW. WHO'S TO SAY HIM BEING OK FUCKING ME WITHOUT ONE, HES NOT DOING THE SAME WITH OTHERS?" I shouted and rolled my eyes.

"Why you mad at me? I'm just stating the obvious."

"I'm not mad at you. I'm mad at myself for liking someone based off his looks and sex game. I don't even know him personally, yet; I fell victim to unprotected sex and him hurting my feelings already."

"Are you going to continue fucking him?"

"You instilled a lot in me growing up, even if it wasn't in the correct way." She did tell me about the birds and the bees but it went more along the lines of, *if you sleep with a guy make sure he wears a condom because I ain't helping you raise no bad ass kids. And if you get a disease, make sure me or your dad are on your life insurance policy in case you die.* Yea, she had a way with words.

"If I do, I'll make sure one of us is wearing protection."

"Good to know."

I stomped up the steps and wiped the tears falling down my face. No matter how strong I was on the streets, she is the only one who could break me down. She knew which buttons to push and I hated it. I locked the door to my bedroom, hopped in the shower and laid down. I made sure to clean up my sex toys first though. My mother doesn't need to see what I do behind closed doors or even assume. She judges me enough about everything else.

Waleed

"Where the fuck you been?" I snatched shorty up from the back.

We were at the club and I only noticed her because she walked in with Khloe and my boy had a fit. Ever since the day I met her, we've been like oil and milk and for some reason, I had to have her. But Risky was becoming obsessed over her friend. She must've thrown it on his ass because he ain't been right ever since he got a taste.

"Nigga what I tell you about touching me?" She tried to move away and I drug her off the seat and to my area.

"Damn, look at all that ass she got." I gave dude a look.

"My bad yo. That's you?" He asked and put his hands up in surrender.

"All motherfucking day. When you see her, know that's me."

"I am not with him." She folded her arms and I pushed her in the dark corner.

"Calm yo thick ass down." I licked my lips as I stared down in the shirt she wore. It crossed in front and her cleavage was on display. It tied in the middle and her bra held her titties up perfect. I wanted to motorboat in those big ass things.

"What you want Waleed?" She peeked around me to see what her girl was doing.

"She cool. My boy won't let nothing happen to her."

"Fuck yo boy." She rolled her eyes looking in his direction.

"Why you say that?"

"He's a bitch ass nigga."

"A bitch ass nigga? How you see that?"

"Over the last few weeks, he's been fucking my girl like crazy. He doesn't want her to leave the house to go out or be with anyone else and yet; he won't dare get caught around her. I mean look. He giving her a deadly stare because some other dude ain't ashamed to be by her." I ran my hand down my face. I specifically told that nigga to leave her alone for this reason right here. Fucking her is one thing but he was tryna lock her down behind closed doors. No, it has nothing to do with me or shorty but it's gonna trickle down. That's her friend and I'd do the same, if she were mine.

"He better not do it." She pushed past me and I followed her. I gave a head nod to the dudes in our crew to watch our back. Whoever Khloe was speaking to had her full attention. She was smiling and my boy wasn't happy.

"Bounce nigga." Risky said and pushed him away from Khloe.

"Ryan what are you doing?" She stood up and his facial expression told it all. Her body was on full display in her outfit. Well not full display but her jeans looked painted on and her flat stomach could be seen under the half shirt.

"Go home Khloe." Now it was her turn to make a face.

"I'm not going no fucking where and why are you over here? Don't you have your trophy wife sitting with you?" She pointed and sure enough Veronica had just made it in our section. She was speaking to someone, who pointed to us.

"Exactly. Get the fuck away from me Ryan."

"Yea Ryan. She doesn't want you or can't you hear?" The dude said and even Khloe gave him a crazy look.

"Hold up nigga. You don't get to talk to him like that."
I couldn't believe she held him down in front of a random.

"Bitch, you weren't just talking that shit before he got here." I knew what was coming next and moved Luna out the way. I wasn't fast enough to move Khloe so she felt Risky's fist to her face; knocking her out. Shit got crazy after that. Mad people were fighting and I couldn't focus on the girls because my gun was on some dudes' head. He tried to sneak Risky and that wasn't happening.

After the cops arrived and everyone dispersed, the only people left were me, Luna, Khloe, who had an ice pack on her face and one of the bodyguards that came with them. I keep asking why he's there but she only said, her dad was a very important man and never allowed her to leave without them. I walked outside with the girls and to the truck.

"Khloe, I know how much you like him but sis you have to move on."

"I know." She put her head down in embarrassment.

"Do you K? Look what he did." I sucked my teeth.

"Yes it was an accident but he had no right to approach you or that guy. Then to make matters worse, you had his back when the dude tried to come for him and he left with the bitch. He didn't even say sorry or check to see if you were ok. Khloe, you deserve so much better." I lit my blunt and blew smoke in the air, as I watched her cry and listened to Luna tell her to leave my boy alone.

"Waleed please don't tell him how upset I am." I looked at her. I was gonna cuss him the fuck out.

"Please. I know we were only sleeping together and I should've left him alone before falling for him but he won't let me."

"What you mean?" She chuckled and Luna rolled her eyes.

"I tried to take a step back but he tells me no. I can't be with anyone and if I even think about it, he'll kill me and the guy. You say it was an accident that he hit me. However, in my eyes, it's his way of telling me he meant everything he said."

"Nah. He's not a woman beater."

"I'm not saying he is and I'm sure it was an accident but he had no business coming over to me."

"I don't disagree with that."

"Look. All I'm saying is, he doesn't want people to know about us but I can't be with anyone. Yet he flaunts his woman in my face." I didn't respond and moved from the truck. I told Luna to come by me. I no longer wanted to hear the shit Risky was doing because it was pissing me off and I don't even know her like that.

"Put your number in my phone and I swear if it's the wrong one, I'ma fuck you even harder the first time."

"Well in that case, maybe I should give you the wrong one." She smirked and stuffed the phone in my jeans after doing it.

"Come home with me."

"Waleed, let me take her home and I'll call you." She stood on her tippy toes and slid her tongue in my mouth. My arms wrapped around her ass and I squeezed it.

"Mmmmmm. I'm gonna give you what you want later." She ran her hands up and down my chest.

"Hurry up and bring yo sexy ass over." I kissed her again and watched her get in the truck. Ima tear that ass up, when I get it.

****

I had the music blasting on my way to see Luna because she didn't wanna come to my place. I was supposed to hit Risky up and see what the hell he was doing but he turned his phone off. We spoke every day and not once did he mention falling in love with, or even fucking Khloe on a reg. He couldn't tell me he wasn't falling for her because Lacey had the same effect on him. He may have been with Veronica and loved her but it was nothing like this. I mean he rocked a nigga over Khloe and she wasn't even doing anything with him.

I knew he had hit it a few other times after showing her dad the house and that was weeks ago but Luna said he still is. What I didn't understand is why he's ashamed of her. Shit, I snatched Luna's chunky ass up and made sure everyone knew to back up. I know he doesn't have to be like me but damn, the look on Khloe's face was sad and disappointing. Not only did he bounce, he took Veronica with him and didn't check on her and that's fucked up. I know for a fact he didn't mean to hit her but I also understand where she was coming from too. This nigga won't allow her to fuck with anyone but he can.

I've never been the nigga to hold a woman back from doing her, especially; if I'm out there doing me. I tried that shit out once with Dora's ass and it didn't work. Yes, I said dirty ass Dora. I don't claim her if I don't have to but I know people will read this and ask questions.

She was Ronny's friend and yes, we were fucking on a regular at one time. I never allowed anyone to know about us because she had a lot of immature ways about her and I hated it. I did give that bitch any and everything her heart desired but it wasn't enough. She wanted a baby, a house and a marriage. Shit, that was after four months. In my eyes, it wasn't enough time for me to decide if being locked down was for me. I was young, Risky had just turned the business to me and I knew it would take a lotta time away from her.

Anyway, she grew inpatient after the first year and moved herself in my crib, purchased a whole bunch of shit without my knowledge. It wasn't a problem but when the bitch

119

bought a truck for her momma, things for her siblings and even tried to get a house for her grandmother who was getting evicted, I had to put my foot down. I didn't even like her family and here she was using my money to upgrade them. I cut her ass off and kicked her out. I still been fucking her but not without two condoms at a time. She won't trap my ass.

I parked in front of the address Luna gave me and made sure this was the correct one. The shit was huge. I sent her a text and stepped out to press the button on the gate. Hell yea, she had one and it was a big black iron one. Once she heard my voice, the gate opened and I was even more amazed at the well-kept lawn and circular driveway. Even the lights that graced the walkway were nice. I was mad jealous because my shit was big too but it wasn't this nice. Call me a bitch all you want. I appreciated nice things.

I walked to the door and once it opened my dick was ready to bust out my jeans.

"DAMNNNNNNN!" Luna had on a skin tight, all black shiny catsuit. The heels were high as hell and her

120

makeup was on point. I appreciate fine women too, no matter what their size. She closed the door.

"I see you're ready."

"HELL FUCKING YEA!" She laughed and led me up the stairs.

I tripped going up the steps because I couldn't focus on anything but the ass in front of me. She opened the bedroom door and there were pink and white rose petals, candles burning and slow music playing. The bedroom was red and black and the drapes were the same. She pushed me on the bed and bent down to remove my Timbs. I stared down at her titties tryna pop out. After she stripped me down to everything but my boxers, she stood in front of me.

"What do you want from me Waleed?" She let her tongue flicker in my ear.

"Whatever you tryna give." I let my hands roam her body. She swatted them away and told me to scoot all the way on the bed and let my back touch the headboard. Another song came on, she turned around with her index finger in her mouth and seductively walked to me.

I like it when you lose, I like it when you go there,

I like the way you use it, I like that you don't play fair,

Recipe for disaster, when I'm just tryna take my time,

Stroke is getting deeper and faster, Screaming like I'm

outta line,

Who came to make sweet love, not me?

The song *When We* by Tank played and a nigga was impressed like a motherfucker by how well she moved her body. I'm talking about leg in the air and everything. I studied every move, to make sure when I'm fucking her, she'll be able to go in every position. She climbed on the bed and moved up slowly. I felt her lips kissing in between my thighs and her hands pulled my boxers down. Her eyes popped open and I grinned. A nigga ain't packing no 12-inch dick but I'm pretty big.

"Sssssss woman." Her tongue slid over the tip and I could feel her spit sliding down the shaft.

Shorty had my head gone with the way she stroked, spit, sucked and juggled my balls in her mouth. I was a sucker for head and she was about to have a nigga strung the fuck out on that alone. She started going faster and the nut I tried to hold in began to come up. I was ready to let her swallow. She placed both hands on the side of my legs, continued sucking with no hands and once I started exploding; she grabbed it, sucked for a second or two before letting me cum on her face. The sight was sexy as fuck.

"Mmmmm, you taste real good and I appreciate you giving me my first cum facial. I always wanted to try it." She kissed the tip and left my ass lying there with my mouth hanging open. I heard the water in the bathroom running and a few minutes later she returned patting her face dry with a towel.

"Yo, if you ever do that for anyone else, I promise to knock your fucking teeth out." I sat up and pulled her closer.

"At least the guy won't have to worry about my teeth scratching him up." I don't know why hearing her mentioning another nigga pissed me off but it did. I stood up and pushed her against the wall and that wasn't an easy task because she kept tryna push me away and she was strong as hell.

"Take this shit off." I unzipped the suit and smiled. Luna was on the plus size but she wasn't 600 pounds either. She had a stomach but you could tell by her legs, she worked out a little. Not that it mattered because she was still getting the D.

"You think because you sucked the shit outta my dick, you can talk shit." I bent my knees, lifted her ass up, stuck my dick inside and probably fell in love at the same time. Her pussy was tight, gushy and kept squeezing the fuck outta me.

"Waleed, I'm sorry. Shit, baby you feel so fucking good." Her nails were in my back and her head was against the wall. My arms were getting a little tired so I put her down and bent her over the dresser. I was going insane as I hit it from the back. Her ass was jiggling, she was throwing it back and I was about to cum.

"I'm cumming ma."

"Then do it nigga." She bent over to touch her ankles and instead of cumming, I pulled out. My dick was mad I stopped.

"What the fuck you doing?"

"You talk too much shit. Come here." She walked to me and I made her stand against the wall.

"Lift that leg to your shoulder." I could see her wetness dripping and as bad as I wanted to drink it up, I had to show her who was boss.

"Oh FUCKKKKKKKKKKKK! Waleed, I can't…"

"You can take it baby. Damn, you wetting my dick up." I saw her body shake and her cream coating my entire dick.

"Yessssss." She came again and her legs were weakening.

"You done talking shit?"

"Yea baby." I let her leg down and sat back on the bed. She was about to get on her knees but I made her get on all fours and put my head in that pussy. Her ass was huge but it didn't stop me from tasting her sweetness and I'm glad I did. She had a strawberry taste to her and I couldn't get enough. I

125

let her sit on my face and I could tell she was nervous but hell, she wasn't as big as she thought.

"I'm cumming ma." I told her after she slid on top of my dick. She rode me like a damn jockey. It wasn't nothing she couldn't do.

"Me too. Fuckkkkk. Yessss." Her body shook and she tried to get off before I came but I held her there. I wasn't tryna get a disease or get her pregnant but it felt way too good, to pull out. She fell on the side of me and I had my arm over my head. Risky said, big women had good pussy but Luna's is beyond good. I pulled her close to me, wrapped my arms around her and fell asleep. Now that's how you put a nigga to bed.

Veronica

"Girl, I don't know what the hell is wrong with him. All I know is he knocked the fat bitch out."

"Did you at least beat her ass?" Dora was grilling me hard about last night. I guess the chaos made the news and since she wasn't there, I was the eyewitness for her.

"Hell no. I tried to kick her in the face while she was on the ground but Risky picked me up and made us leave." I watched the fight going on and after finding a way to get the fat bitch, my foot was about to stomp on her face. I was pissed he stopped me.

"Hmph. You think he fucking her?"

"I doubt it but even if he is, I bet he'll never claim her."

"Hell no. Risky isn't about to ruin his reputation for her." She said and was right. He had standards.

"Shit, that nigga loves his trophy wife." I told her.

"Bitch, you ain't his wife." I sucked my teeth at her comment. So what I wasn't his wife. I'm gonna be her one day and until then, he'll be mine.

"Yet. And still, he prides his self on having a bad bitch on his arm at all times."

"That is true. Anyway, let me tell you about Lamar's ass." I braced myself for the conversation that was bound to last at least an hour. Once she told you a story, it went on and on.

Ding Dong!

"Hold on bitch. Somebody is at his door."

"You not waking him up?"

"For what? After fucking last night, he's knocked out. Shit, the only reason I'm up is because I had to use the bathroom and your aggy ass called."

"Fuck you heffa." I went to the door and made sure the T-shirt I wore was low enough to cover my ass. Not that I'm worried about anything but he would have a fit if anyone saw my goodies. I opened the door and smiled. She stood there with a big Louis Vuitton duffle bag and a smaller one. *Was he staying at her house?*

"Ummm, is Ryan here?"

"I know that bitch isn't at his door." I heard Dora screaming in my ear.

"Ryan?" I knew she meant Risky but why was she addressing him by his real name? I didn't even call him that.

"If you mean Risky, he's in the bed. After the night we had, I doubt he'll be up anytime soon."

"Oh ok." She lifted the sunglasses up.

"Damn, he did that to your face?" I guess she forgot about the mark and obviously didn't care because she kept the glasses on top of her head. I smirked and Dora's dumb ass, asked me to take a picture. So of course, I pretended to text and took a few. Not sure which one would actually come out because I wasn't able to take a clear shot without her noticing.

"Yup, which is why I'm bringing his things here."

"Where did you get this?" She dropped the bags at my feet.

"Maybe you should ask him."

"I'm asking you. Were you fucking him?" She slid the sunglasses back on her face and turned to leave.

"Again, you should ask him."

"I don't even know why I asked. He's told me a few times he'd never fuck or be with a fat bitch. He has a reputation to protect and no one is messing it up." Her body swung around to face me.

"That's good to know but let me fill you in on a secret." She stepped in my personal space.

"Ask your man why he was fighting a man who tried talking to me? I mean, why was Ryan even around me when he had you? Fat bitches can make his stock drop, right? Its funny how a man can say so many things one day, make you believe it and then disrespect and treat you like shit the next, just to save face. What do you think Ryan?" I turned around and he was standing there looking dumbfounded.

"Have a good day." She went to step off the porch and moved past me.

"Khloe?"

"Be careful Ryan. You don't want her to snap a photo of you speaking to a fat bitch." I gave her a fake smile.

"I'm sorry for…" She put her hand up and removed her glasses.

"What are you sorry for? Knocking me out like a nigga off the street, or acting like a fool because I was talking to another man?" He let his hand run over his head. The black eye and swollen face did look bad.

"I know it was an accident but nothing you say will ever make me forgive you for leaving me at the club. The least you could have done was made sure I was alright before running off into the sunset with her." She pointed to me and I gave her a cute little wave.

"I didn't mean to. I…" Was he really tryna explain to her?

"It doesn't matter anymore. You made it clear enough that fat bitches aren't who you see yourself with. Goodbye." She stood on her tippy toes and kissed his cheek.

"KHLOE!" He shouted but she got in her nice ass truck and peeled out. He better not had brought her that and he re-poed mine.

He snatched the bags up off the floor and stormed upstairs. From the looks of things, it appeared he definitely was fucking her. But was he falling for her? No, he couldn't be.

131

I closed the door and went upstairs to find him in the shower. When he gets angry it always made the sex better and right now he is. He had his back against the wall as the water hit him, like he was in deep thought. I wasted no time stripping and joining. He didn't acknowledge me stepping in and stayed in place. I kneeled down and took him in my mouth. I had to get his focus back on me right now. We were doing fine last night and I'll be damned if her pissing him off, stops our shopping trip he promised. Say what you want, but a bitch was in dire need of new clothes, shoes and everything else he used to buy me.

After he threw me out, I went to the bank with the 5k he knew was missing and placed it in an account. I already had a few hundred thousand in there from all the times he gave me money. My momma didn't raise no fool. I got me a one-bedroom condo and furnished it right away. I even went out and brought me a brand-new Ford Escape truck. It's far from the Bentley car and BMW truck he took but at least it was mine.

"Shit, K." He mumbled but I still heard him. I would've stopped if the shopping trip wasn't on my mind. Was I hurt? Yup, but I also knew he could fantasize about her all he wants, she'll never be on his arm and that's a fact.

"Thanks." He said and grabbed the soap to wash.

"Are you going to return the favor?" Ever since he started fucking me again, he refused to go down and I didn't know why. Risky had a way with his tongue to drive a bitch insane. Hell, its another reason I'm still here.

"Nope!" He had venom in his voice. Instead of pissing him off or catching an attitude, I left it alone and washed up.

"You coming or not?" He barked when I got out the shower. His ass left me in there and was already dressed.

"Hold on."

"If you're not ready in five minutes, I'm out." My ass rushed and was down in four. Call me money hungry all you want but my ass was gonna get some new shit.

****

It took him a while to clear his attitude but once he did, we were fine. He walked in every store with me and I caught

133

him looking at women's clothes that weren't my size. Again, as long as he's funding me, I don't give a fuck. I also know he won't purchase anything if I'm here. He may not care what I think but he does for others. I never understood why and I guess, I'll never know because I didn't give a fuck.

"Damn, I missed you Khloe." I heard and he must've too because we both turned around.

"Its been a long time." She gave him a hug and he didn't wanna let her go. Risky's face was turned up and if he could attack, he would.

"How are the kids?"

"Getting big. I see you're still with your crazy ass friend." He pointed to the big light skinned chick who was grilling the fuck outta us.

"Why do you have sunglasses on in here?" I saw Risky's facial expression change when the guy asked her. You could tell he felt bad.

"Oh, there was a fight at the club last night and I was in the way." She shrugged and the light skinned chick came in our direction.

"Luna, where you going?" Once she saw us her entire demeanor changed to sad. I guess seeing me with him and all the bags only verified we were indeed together.

"If you even think about acting stupid, I'll shoot you in your dick and you know I will." He chuckled at the Luna chick.

"And I told you not to play those tough games with me." He stood behind her and his arm was around her throat.

"She got five seconds to walk the fuck away from that nigga or its gonna be a problem." He pushed her away and she shook her head.

"You're ok with a nigga stalking my best friend?" She asked me and I shrugged my shoulders.

"He's not stalking her."

"I guess you would say that being he's funding this shopping trip. Stupid ass bitch." I stood up and Risky gave me a look to calm down.

"You're a fucking asshole and I hope she never speaks to you again." She walked off and those words must've hurt because he was livid.

I think it was more because the Khloe chick had disappeared as well. What the hell type of pussy control did this bitch have on my man? I had to get rid of her soon. Otherwise; he'll never take me back.

Luna

"What the hell is going on Luna?" My dad bombarded me with questions the moment I walked through the door.

"I don't know what you mean." I put my purse and keys on the table in the foyer area and walked in the kitchen. My mom stayed in here cooking.

"Hola mami." I kissed her cheek and felt my body being jerked.

"I'm talking to you."

"Carlos, don't put your hands on my daughter. I'll smack the shit outta you." My dad didn't play with my mom.

"Whatever."

"What's the problem dad?"

"The problem is, you aren't spending time with Oscar?" I rolled my eyes and took a seat at the table.

"I don't want to." My mom placed the spoon on the stove, wiped her hands on the apron and took a seat next to me.

"Honey, you know this has to happen." She said and rubbed my back.

"Why do I have to marry him? We're not in love and he's a fucking asshole."

"Watch your mouth young lady." My dad yelled and my mom waved him off like always.

"You have eight months left Luna so if I were you, I'd find a way to love him." My father stormed out the kitchen.

See, my dad is on the verge of retiring from the Cartel and desperately wants me to take over. He didn't have any sons and refuses to give it away, therefore; he wants me or should I say, betrothed me to some guy who is in Mexico being groomed to be by my side to do it. He'll run it because I don't want any parts of it but in order for him to do it, we have to be married before I'm 25. If not, he automatically gets it and regardless of my dad saying he's retiring, he still wants to be involved. It's obvious he can't if I don't marry this guy.

Don't get me wrong, Oscar is a sexy Mexican. His swag is on point and people respected him over there. He also has a ton of women who are flocking to the next head of Cartel, which is going to be him. Mind you, he doesn't love me and has an issue marrying me as well. It's unfortunate that both of our parents did this when we were kids. We had no say so then and none now.

"Luna why don't you wanna marry him?" My mom handed me a napkin to wipe my tears. Every time my dad yelled at me, I'd get emotional. I was a daddy's girl too so it always upset me.

"One... I don't wanna marry someone, I'm not in love with and two..." I looked around to make sure my dad was outta earshot.

"His dick is little." I thought my mom would fall out the chair from laughing so hard.

"It's not pinky little but after being with someone else, there's no way I could turn back."

"Who is he?" She moved the hair out my face.

"Who?"

"The man you're falling for?" I grabbed my phone, turned on the camera and looked at myself.

"What are you doing?"

"Looking to see if love is written on my face." She put her hand on mine and turned me to look at her.

139

"It's not on your face."

"Then how can you tell?"

"Well you never gave your dad this much lip over being married. I mean, you never agreed but lately you've been very combative over it. And two... the smile that graced your face when I asked who he was." I put my head on the table. I felt her staring even if I wasn't looking in her direction.

"Ughhhhhh, he makes me sick."

"Luna. It can't be that bad."

"I'm serious mom. He's such a fucking asshole, he's arrogant, we fight all the time and in Florida, he's the reason I shot Khloe by accident. Then before he leaves, he throws his tongue down my throat and tells me we're definitely going to fuck." My mom covered her mouth.

"I threw the remote at him and he did it back. Then a week ago we finally stopped arguing and took it there." I smiled reminiscing on how he handled me very well. My mom sat there staring without saying a word.

"I know ma. He's crazy but the best part about him is, he doesn't care about my weight and told his entire crew in the club to stay away from me because I'm his." I saw a few tears leaving her eyes.

"Ma, you know Oscar wants me to lose weight so I can resemble those skinny heffas over there. Shit, between him and daddy stressing me, it's the reason I gained so much weight in the first place." It was true. I wasn't always a big girl but over the last six or seven years my dad was pressuring me over getting married. Then Oscar begged me to get skinny. Talking about when I give him kids, I'll get bigger and he doesn't want a humongous wife.

"I want to meet him."

"Daddy is gonna have a fit."

"Let me worry about him. I have to meet the man who finally broke down my daughters' wall." I sucked my teeth.

"I'm serious. Those little boys you messed with never had you like this. You have that happy glow and I'm impressed." I sat there grinning and picked my phone back up.

Big Baby: *Where the hell your sexy, chunky ass at?*

Me: *What I tell you about calling me that?*

Big Baby: *I don't care what you say. You are chunky and sexy as fuck. Now, where you at?*

Me: *You make me sick. I'm at my parents' house."*

Big Baby: *Well hurry up because I need that good ass pussy riding my dick.*

Me: *BYE.* I put the phone down and my mom was over my shoulder cracking up.

"Ma, really?"

"I wanted to know why you were smiling and not answering me and now I see why.

"I'm leaving."

"Yea, you better get over there and ride that dick." My face had to be beet red. Me and my mom discussed a lot but when it came to sex, I tried to keep it PG but as you can see, she doesn't.

"Don't look at me like that. I'm about to throw this pussy on your father to calm him down." I made a gesture like I was throwing up and she tossed the sponge at me. I hopped in my car and went to Waleed's house only to find some bullshit going on.

****

"Hey babe." He said and pulled me in front of him. They were in front of the fence.

"Babe?" The dirty chick from Florida asked. We never discussed being a couple and I'm sure he was being smart so I didn't correct him. Plus, he'd probably put a hurting on my pussy if I did.

After the first night we slept together, he stayed the night, woke me up to sex the next morning and we've been fucking like porn stars ever since. I must say the dick so good he has me ready to pop the question to him.

"Yup that's my girl and if you even think about saying some slick shit, Ima let her slide yo ass before I do it." I smirked.

"Why she here?" I asked and moved closer to him.

"She wanted to fuck but I told her you had that covered." He stuck his hands in my jeans. He loved feeling on my ass.

"That I do." He leaned down to kiss me and outta nowhere shots were fired. He threw me on the ground and dirty Dora stood there screaming.

Waleed chased the truck down the street but you could hear it speeding off. When I walked down there, he was on his phone barking orders. Evidently, he had a partial plate and wanted someone to go through every number. I hate to tell him it was gonna be a while before someone could get him the information. I wrapped my arms around his waist and he placed his hand on mine.

"You good?" He turned and checked me over.

"I'm ok. Your little friend is probably traumatized."

"Fuck her. As long as you good, I'm good."

"Let me find out you getting sweet on the kid."

"I'm definitely sweet on yo ass." He took my hand in his and led me to the house. Dora was gone and he made sure to bring my truck in his driveway. He has a fence around his property too but not like mine. I still felt secure, nonetheless.

"You hungry?" He asked as he texted away on his phone.

"Yea. Can we go out to eat or is it too risky?"

"It's whatever you want. Let me grab my keys." I smiled and felt sad at the same time. Here is a guy who has no problem showing me off to the world. Then I have my friend, who's fucking his and he's ashamed of her. How did I get so lucky? I pulled my phone out my purse and saw the text from Oscar.

Oscar: *I'll be in town soon. We need to meet up.*

Me: *I'll be here.* I looked to my left and Waleed was staring at me.

"What's up?"

"You better not be texting another nigga."

"When you get rid of your ho's, I'll get rid of my niggas." I started laughing and he yanked me by the hair.

"I play a lotta fucking games but sharing pussy ain't one of them."

"Get off me." He gripped my hair tighter.

"I'm not the nigga to fuck with Luna. Look me up if you don't believe me." I didn't say a word because little did he know, I already did.

145

I learned Risky worked at a funeral home and was a killer by night. Waleed ran the drug business now and he is just as deadly as his friend, if not worse. And I say worse because some of the stories are very horrific. It intrigued me to mess with someone as dangerous as my dad but now that he's showed me a little anger, I wasn't so sure if I'm willing to deal with it.

Waleed

"Take me back to my truck." She said after I released her hair.

"Nope."

"Fuck this. I'll jump out."

"Go head and see how far you get." Of course, I was testing her to see if she'd really do it.

"Fuck you." She unlocked the door and I watched as she waited for me to stop. The light had just turned yellow and I could see her hand on the knob.

"Don't wait for me to stop. Do it now." I pressed hard on the pedal and sped through the light.

"Hurry up and get out."

"I hate you." She had her arms folded on her chest.

"Already. Damn, I'm offended." She started punching me in the arm and even caught me a few times in my chest.

"Don't ever put your hands on me again." She screamed out. I slammed on the brakes and heard cars honking their horns. I stared and she had a few tears coming down her face.

"What's really good? You can't be that mad I pulled your hair."

"Hell yea I am. Then you say I can't text other men, when I know for a fact you still entertain bitches. Got damn asshole." Her face was beet red and my dick was hard. I finally moved over, put the car in park and went to her side. She didn't wanna open the door but lucky for me I had the key.

"Look at me." She turned her head away.

"Luna, I apologize for pulling your hair and as long as I'm not fucking these bitches, don't let shit bother you. But I meant what I said, about you not texting other niggas."

"You sound stupid."

"Oh yea." I forced her to turn around, put my face in her neck and bit down.

"Owww. Stop Waleed, it hurts." She was tryna push me off.

"I'm serious about us being exclusive Luna."

"But you have other chicks calling your phone."

148

"If it's gonna be a problem, Ima block everyone. Look." I pulled my phone out, hit the block button on every chick and then deleted their names from my phone. I only called them when I was horny and since she's satisfying me, there's no need to speak to them.

"Feel better?" I leaned in to kiss her and she let her hand slip in my jeans.

"You better had." I felt her massaging my dick and as always, he'd rise to the occasion for her.

"Take those jeans off." I pointed to hers.

"Baby, not here."

"There's no one out here ma and I need a quickie or something. Shit, I'd be blowing your back out if you weren't hungry." She seemed nervous as I unbuttoned her pants and slipped them under her ass.

"Babe, I'm not a skinny chick and..." I already had one leg out, slid her panties to the side and gave her something to calm down. It really was a quickie because I didn't want anyone watching us.

"Always good baby." I kissed her lips, pulled my jeans up and closed her door. I monitored my surroundings the entire time and no one paid us any mind.

"Here." I reached in the glove box and passed her some napkins.

"What we eating?

"I wanna go to sleep." She struggled pulling her jeans up but she did it.

"Hell no. You got me out here, so what's it gonna be?" I stared over at her and her eyes were closed. I shook my head laughing. She always talking shit and pass out each time she gets a good nut. I parked in the drive thru of Popeye's, ordered our food and took us to my house.

"Come on." I tapped her leg and she jumped.

"I'm tired."

"You know damn well I'm not carrying your chunky ass." She smacked me on the arm.

"Why do you call me that?" I grabbed her hand and we walked in the house.

"Because you're thick as hell and the word thickums is overused in the streets. I want my own name for you and I'll never call you fat, so chunky it is." I locked the door and headed to the kitchen.

"Do you think I'm fat?" She dug her food out the bag.

"No but that pussy sure is." She tossed a fry at me.

"It is but on some real shit, you're not fat. Do you have extra meat on your body? Absolutely! Do you weigh more than the average woman? Probably! But it's the reason why I want you. The reason, I'm not letting you go." I saw the smile creep on her face. As a man, we knew when a woman wanted or needed attention and it was up to us, to give it. Otherwise; the next man in her ear will take her away and it won't be shit you can do.

"Why because fat girls don't cheat and men aren't insecure with them?" I stood in front of her.

"Luna, I'm sure you heard a lotta motherfuckers talk about your weight growing up and I get you're comfortable in your own skin but don't try and get in my head. There's much more to you than a clothes size and to start, it's that pussy and head game." She pushed me away.

"And it's the way you take pride in who you are. You're not out here tryna pretend to be something you're not. Your confidence is over 1000% and I love that shit because it means you won't allow anyone to make you feel less of a woman." She put her head down and I lifted it back up.

"Luna, it's women out here who wish they had the same fuck you attitude as you but are too scared to show it. It may be early but a nigga is proud to have you by his side and that's some real shit."

"Will you marry me?" She asked and we both busted out laughing.

"Even if this don't work out between us, just know we'll always be friends and I got you for life." I told her and that was the God's honest truth. She was more than a person I'm having sex with. My feelings were definitely involved and by the way she acts, I know she has some towards me as well.

"You do huh?"

"Damn right." She fed me one of her fries.

"Waleed, there's something I need to tell you." I could see the seriousness in her face.

"Hold on ma." I picked my phone up for Risky and ended up talking a lot longer than expected. By the time I finished, Luna had showered and fell asleep in my bed, which is exactly where I wanted her.

****

"Nigga, what the fuck were you thinking punching Khloe and even attacking the dude she was talking to?" This is the first time we discussed the night at the club. We were both wrapped up in a lotta shit but tonight we were out drinking. Luna was somewhere with Khloe anyway so I didn't have anything to do.

"Man, I can't even tell you. I saw her smiling and happy, and sad to say, it pissed me off. All I can say is, I should've listened to you."

"About?" I lifted my beer.

"Leaving Khloe alone."

153

"You never did listen when I talked." He and I always gave each other advice but neither of us ever listened to the other and would always end up in some craziness.

"What the fuck ever. How about Ronny gets in the shower, starts giving me head and I say K's name?"

"Oh shit. What she say?"

"Nothing. She kept going like I knew she would." I looked at him.

"I promised to take her shopping."

"Figured." Veronica is a money hungry bitch and regardless of how many times Risky would curse her out, or even disrespect her, she'd still be there. She knew he'd give her what she wanted and if dealing with his attitude here and there is all it took to get shit from him, she dealt with it.

"Then, I almost flipped out in the mall when I saw K hugging some dude." I looked at him crazy. This nigga was probably already in love with her but fighting it due to her weight.

"Nigga, if you don't stop faking the funk and go get your woman."

"She ain't my woman and the pussy may be good but I'm Aight."

"Only a nigga in love acts this way." I told him and he tossed some napkins at me.

"Fuck you." I shook my head laughing.

"Long time, no see." I turned around and there was Julie. Another bitch I couldn't stand.

"What you want?"

"Can I talk to you outside for a minute?" She asked and I told her no because I was with my boy.

"Go head man. I'm about to leave anyway. I'll hit you tomorrow when I hear back from dude." We slapped hands.

"Peace out Julie." He gave her a hug and left. She took a seat next to me.

"I miss you." I felt her hand on my shoulder.

"Bye Julie." I stood up, paid for my tab and walked out.

"WALEED! I'm sorry." I turned around.

"Sorry for what? Getting rid of my baby or fucking another nigga right after?"

"All of it. Waleed, I was scared and.-"

"And so was I but I wouldn't have left you. Then you fuck a dude you know I'm around all the time."

"Cut the shit Waleed. You and Lamar can't stand each other."

"Not the fucking point. Would you be ok with me doing that to you?"

"You already did." I heard her mumble but she refused to elaborate on it.

"What do you really want? I know it's not to tell me about some baby you kept from me because I found you at the clinic and saw the papers. So why are you here after all this time?" She caught me off guard with the kiss and instead of stopping her, I continued for a few seconds.

"Nah, this ain't happening." I pushed her off when my dick started growing.

Real quick; Julie is an ex, I was madly in love with. We were young, she got pregnant, aborted the baby and fucked Lamar a couple of weeks later. I was pissed about the abortion but when I asked why she slept with him, she said because I cheated on her, when in fact I didn't.

If you're wondering, yes, I knew Lamar way before Risky and his sister got together. He's always been a grimy nigga so I didn't expect loyalty from him. However, she was on some fuck shit and I couldn't move past it.

"Why not? I see you miss me."

"Not at all. My dick got hard because you kissed me but don't get it fucked up. I don't want you." She stuck her hands in my jeans and pulled my man out.

"Yo, you bugging." I pushed her out the way, closer my door and pulled off. *Whew!* I had to get away from her before she got what she wanted and I couldn't do that to Luna.

Khloe

"Are you ok?" I asked the person in the next stall. I was at Red Lobster with my dad because he wanted seafood but nothing expensive. When I came in to use the bathroom, I heard someone throwing up.

"I'm ok." It sounded like a kid but I couldn't be sure. The person continued throwing up until you heard dry heaving. The toilet flushed and shortly after, the door I opened. I was at a loss for words when a young girl stepped out. She moved around me, washed her hands, rinsed her mouth out and grabbed a paper towel for her face. Her eyes were red and you could tell she was crying.

"Are you sick? Do you have food poisoning?" I asked because she didn't look good at all.

"Move your fat ass out the way." My mouth fell open.

"Why are you even here? Shouldn't you be at a buffet? One of your thighs, are the size of my entire body." I snatched her little ass up and threw her against the wall. I had no business putting my hands on someone's kid but her mouth was reckless.

"Listen here Heffa." I said and placed my hands on my hips.

"Heffa."

"You heard me." I yoked her up by the shirt.

"Get your hands off me." She tried prying them off but I had a death grip on her.

"I stayed in here to make sure you were ok. The least you can do is say thank you."

"Did I ask you?" This little bitch was about to make me smack the shit outta her.

"I see your momma raised a disrespectful little girl. Your father probably in jail and you out stealing." I stared at the expensive ass Jordan's and her clothes even seemed to cost a lot. I doubt she's stealing but these days, you never know.

"I don't need to steal because my daddy is rich and bitch you don't know me."

"I don't have to. Your mouth is disgusting and matter of fact, who you here with? Is your momma out there?"

159

"No." She rolled her eyes and her neck.

"And why not? She needs to know why her daughter is about to get her ass beat in this bathroom. I don't give a fuck how old you are." I had my arms folded across my chest. And that's when she broke down. I watched her slide to the ground and everything in me said to leave this little bitch but my heart wouldn't let me.

"My mom died when I was five and my daddy is working." I covered my mouth and instantly felt bad.

"Do you want me to get someone?"

"NO!" She shouted and I saw fear on her face.

"You've been in here for a while now. You don't think they'll be worried?"

"No. She probably knows what I'm doing. I promised to stop but I can't." I had no idea who she was talking about.

"Stop what?"

"What you think?" She looked at me like I'm supposed to know what she's talking about.

"Little girl, you're pushing it."

"My bad. People make fun of my weight and..." I didn't even wanna hear the rest but she continued. She mentioned kids bothering her at school and some other things that I couldn't figure out. I'm not sure if she was holding back or what but whatever it is, had a direct effect on her and not in a good way.

A few different women walked in and kept asking if she were ok. It wasn't until an older woman stepped in did she stand up.

"Did someone teach you how to do that?" I asked and she was about to answer.

"Who the fuck are you and why are you questioning my granddaughter." I figured out why her mouth is reckless.

"Well, I came in and your precious granddaughter here..." I stopped when the little girl gave me pleading eyes not to say anything.

"I'm sorry sweetie but that's not a secret I can keep." I told her grandmother and she started crying. I ran out the bathroom and told my dad to keep eating and I'll be out. I was talking to someone I knew.

"They won't stop bothering me at school nana and she said if I get skinny, they'll stop."

"Who told you that?" I asked and closed the door.

"My daddy's girlfriend, well ex. She said, I'm fat and the reason we don't go out as much is because my dad is ashamed. I don't want him to be upset or.-" I stood in front of her.

"I was you at the age of fourteen and I can tell you, you're doing more damage to your body than you think."

"I am."

"Yes. See I thought in order to be friends with kids, I had to be their size but it's not true. If they wanna be your friend they won't care about your weight."

"I keep telling her that." Her grandmother said wiping her eyes. I guess this was affecting her as well.

"People who bully others only do it because they don't feel good about themselves. As far as your dads' girlfriend, you should tell him. I don't think he'll be ok finding out she taught you how to stick your finger down your throat or doing anything possible to be skinny. It's not worth it." She gave me a hug and apologized for disrespecting me. I was shocked and satisfied.

"Let me talk to this woman real quick." Her grandmother said and the little girl stepped out the door. She kept it open to watch her.

"I know it's a lot to ask but can I please have your number in case she wants to talk."

"Umm." I wasn't comfortable giving her my information because it's clear the girl has issues.

"Please. She won't talk to the psychiatrist or her father. She's shut down and we can barely get her to leave the house. You're the first person she's opened up to besides me and since you can relate, it'll be good for her."

"Ok but if she disrespects me again."

"She won't." I stored my number in her phone and went to sit with my dad, who was fucking his crablegs up.

"Sorry about that daddy." He waved me off and the two of us stayed in there for another hour.

He told me how my mom was bugging because he left and the divorce will be finalized in thirty days. He also said, she's trying her hardest to figure out his new address. She will call him over and give him a ton of sex, which was lacking as my dad says. So now he goes to see her when he wants some and she happily obliges. My mom is so used to being with him, she even has him staying on the phone until she falls asleep. Maybe they're better living separate. Whatever the case, my dad was happy and that's all I cared about.

****

"Get it boo." Luna was egging me on the dance floor. We were out at the club celebrating me getting another promotion. My job loved me and with this new position, I cut down on two accounting jobs because I was making more money. I still had two left. You can never have too much money but at least I wasn't over working myself anymore.

"Awww shit girl. There's your song." Motorsport came on and Cardi B's part played. We sung like Offset was our nigga.

"Did the fat girls have a reunion?" This chick said and we turned around to see the one person both of us never cared for.

164

"Move the fuck on before I beat your ass like the old days." Luna said to her sister. Yes, her sister. She never talks about her because they hated one another.

"Still fat though."

"And I'll still put you in the hospital though." I stood in between the two because I hated to see them fight. Well I hated to see Luna rock her to sleep.

"Keep thinking your life is perfect. I can't wait until you get exactly what you deserve." She smirked and walked out.

"What's wrong?" Waleed came over to see what the commotion was. He was out celebrating with us but stepped away to use the phone.

"Nothing babe. I'm good. Everything ok?" He leaned down to kiss her and my heart melted.

In the last few months they've been holding it down and a bitch envied everything about their relationship. Granted he still hasn't asked her to be his woman but in my mind, he doesn't have to because everyone knows it.

"Turn around." Luna had a smirk on her face, while Waleed had a snarl. He wanted me to be with his boy of course, however, Ryan had Ronny to occupy his time.

"Hey Marcus? I'm glad you could make it." I hugged him and we took a seat.

After he fucked me over all those years ago, I finally forgave him. We will never be together as a couple but we can still be friends. It was actually a good feeling letting all the anger and hate go, I had for him. It only consumed me and now that its not, the two of us spoke on the phone a few days out the week. He knew about my promotion and offered to come help celebrate. I waved the waitress over and she brought us a few drinks. We laughed, danced and cracked jokes throughout the night and it felt like old times.

"GET THE FUCK UP!" I turned around and Ryan stood there making my panties wet. He was so damn fine and his hazel eyes pierced straight through me.

"Bye Ryan." Marcus gave me a weird look.

"Bro, you got less than five seconds to get out this seat and beat it." He put a gun to Marcus head and both of us stood.

166

"What's going on Khloe?" Marcus asked and honestly, I couldn't answer because I had no idea why Ryan was being childish. I pushed Ryan back so Marcus could go.

"I'll call you later. I'm so sorry about this."

"If you answer her call, I'll find out and murk you and your kids." Ryan still had the gun pointed at him and shockingly no one did a thing. Its like they were ok with him being reckless.

"Oh my God. What the fuck is wrong with you?" I snapped and attempted to storm past but he grabbed my arm.

"Let's go." He grabbed my purse and phone and led me out the door. I could hear Luna screaming for him to let me go but Waleed must've kept her from coming behind me.

"Get in." There was a black truck with tinted windows in front of me.

"I have my own car. Thank you very much."

"Did I say you had a choice?" I stood there.

"I'm not gonna say it again." He stood behind me and it's sad to say, but his warm breath on the back of my neck enticed the wetness in between my legs. I opened the door and got in. He had someone driving us and they stopped in front of my house.

"Thanks for the ride." He nodded, got out behind me and followed me to the porch.

"You can go now." I was more than aggravated and all I wanted to do was go to sleep.

He closed the door, locked it and made his way up the stairs. I watched him strip outta his clothes and I swear, my ass could cum off his sexy ass body. He came over to me, stripped mine off and led me in the shower. As much as I didn't wanna do this, my body betrayed me with the first kiss.

Risky

Waleed called to tell me he was stepping out with the girls because Khloe got a promotion at her job. Of course, I wanted to see her since she's been avoiding my calls and messages. Hell, she's been staying with her pops just so I won't show up. I didn't wanna disrespect him and gave her the space she wanted. The sad part is I still couldn't find it in me to be with her in public but my body was feenin for her touch. I wanted to feel her lips on mine and witness those beautiful facial expressions she made when I made her cum. To be honest, I missed the hell outta her.

When I walked in and seen her and the nigga at the booth laughing and smiling, it infuriated me. I knew he was her ex and I also knew he wanted her back. Evidently, he proposed to Khloe some years back but messed up and got some chick pregnant; twice. They broke up and now he was here tryna make up for lost time. Call me selfish and any other name you want but no one is going to bed her but me and I mean that shit.

"Did you miss me K?" We were now out the shower and in the bedroom.

"Yessss. Shit yessss." And just like that her body succumbed to another powerful orgasm.

"I missed you too baby." I placed kisses on her entire body and went in for the kill. Her hand was on my head and she was fucking the hell outta my face. After giving her a couple more, I laid on my back and allowed her to ride me and it was one hell of a ride.

"I'm cumming baby." She was bouncing up and down. My fingers circled her clit as her eyes rolled.

"Me too ma."

"Fuckkkkkk. I love you." She screamed out and I held her there as I came. You damn right I'm about to trap her with a baby. When I said no one else will bed her, I meant it. She laid on the floor next to me and I grabbed the covers off the bed and put them on us. This isn't the first time we've slept down here after sex and probably won't be the last. A few minutes later I heard her snoring lightly.

"I love you too K." I kissed the back of her neck and dozed off right behind her. I know it was a sucker move to say it as she slept but I didn't want her thinking other things. Me loving her won't change my perception of being seen with her on public.

****

BANG! BANG! BANG! BANG! I heard and jumped up. K, was still knocked out but someone was banging on her door. I glanced at my phone and not only was it six thirty in the damn morning, there were over twenty missed calls from Ronny. I was supposed to go over her house but my plans changed.

I threw my jeans on and walked down the steps to find Khloe's bitch ass mother on the sofa drinking coffee like she didn't hear the damn door. All the times she's stopped by when I was here, she'd be rude and mean to K. I got in her ass a few times over it and to my knowledge she no longer did it. Well, not when I'm around anyway.

"You couldn't get that?" I asked on my way to the door.

"What for? It's not for me or Khloe." At this very moment, I knew it was about to be some problems. I blew my breath, opened the door and stepped on the porch. We stood there for a good five minutes not saying a word.

"Are you fucking serious Risky?" Ronny was tapping her foot.

"What are you talking about?"

"You fucking this fat bitch? You're staying the night and shit. What the hell?" She was loud as hell and I hoped K didn't hear her.

"No I'm not fucking her. You know I don't fuck fat bitches."

"Then why are you here?"

"Mannn, she was drunk last night so I brought her home and fell asleep on the couch. If you don't believe me ask her mom, who's sitting in there." I opened the door to prove a point and saw a teary-eyed Khloe standing there shaking her head. *FUCK!*

"Well get your things so we can go. If her mom is here, she no longer needs you." I never took my eyes off Khloe and my heart broke when she slid down the wall, with her knees to her chest and started crying hysterical. I fucked up royally. I've always told her; her weight didn't bother me and it doesn't. However, I can't be with her the way she wants so I keep my feelings hidden so I don't confuse her.

Her mom sat there with her nose turned up and disgust on her face. The entire time I got in her ass about disrespecting Khloe and I did it. I'm no better than her or these motherfuckers off the street.

"Khloe?" I reached out for her and she moved away.

"Don't you fucking touch me."

"Fuck her Risky. Come on, I'm hungry and we're supposed to go shopping." Khloe shook her head, wiped her eyes, jumped up off the floor, and stormed up the steps. I took the bitch shopping once since we broke up and now she thinks I'm gonna be doing it all the time. *Yea right.* I only did it because I was mad at Khloe but it won't happen again.

"Goodbye Ryan and take your shit with you." She said coming back down.

"Ok but where is it?" I wanted to smack Ronny for opening her mouth. I didn't ask her to answer for me. She pointed outside and I ran out the door. All my stuff was spread out on the lawn. When the hell did she do this? I was about to go back in but she slammed the door in my face. I picked my things up and walked behind Ronny. I had no choice but to drive home with her because I let one of my boys drop us off last night.

"What you want to eat?" This bitch was all chipper.

"I don't have no clothes on. Take me home." She looked at me and sucked her teeth. How the hell she mad when its her fault? I guess its not all her fault but she had no business bringing her ass over here in the first place.

"Why did you come over here and how did you know where she lived?"

"Oh, I have a tracker on your phone." She said the shit with ease.

"Bitch, are you crazy?" She stopped the car short and I jerked forward.

"Ryan, the two of us have been together for four years and if you think I'm gonna let a fat bitch come in and take what's mine, you're sadly mistaken." I chuckled at her, sent a text on my phone and opened the door.

"Why are you so threatened by the fat woman? Huh? You claim she can't take what's yours but let me be clear about one thing." I stepped out.

"That woman you're so threatened by, has fucked the shit outta me numerous times and I know you're aware because I called you by her name as you sucked my dick. Any other woman would've caused a scene and left. But not you. You're so thirsty, you allowed my money to blind you. I never should've took you shopping that day but I needed to get her off my mind."

"Risky, she'll never be me."

"Nah she won't but one thing's clear and that's, that her pussy has me ready to put a ring on it." The way her mouth hit the ground made me smile. I almost proposed to Veronica but it never happened so I know what I said just hurt her.

"Now you have a good day, ya hear." I slammed the door and hopped in Waleed's truck. I sent him a text when I first got in her car and then again on the way to my house. Something told me to have him come the exact way we were going in case some shit kicked off and I'm happy, I did.

"What she do now?" He handed me the blunt and pulled off. Veronica was still sitting there. It looked as if she were crying but her tears no longer moved me. However, seeing Khloe cry did something to me and I had to figure out a way to make it up to her.

"The bitch showed up at Khloe's and I fucked up tryna keep my relationship with K on the low." I finished telling him everything and he sat there shaking his head.

I know he didn't approve and if my mother knew, she'd be cursing me the fuck out. They don't know one another but still. The issues with my daughter and dealing with her weight problems that Ronny instilled on her should make me leave her alone but I couldn't. Four years is a long time and I did love Veronica. Its like no matter what I did or said, she had a hold on me. I need to free myself from her before moving forward with Khloe, even if it is behind closed doors.

"Man, you need to get over the fear of people seeing you together."

"I know and trust me I want to but how you think Raina will feel?"

"What you mean? Raina don't care who you date." She really doesn't but I also don't want her seeing me move from woman to woman either.

"Ok, say she finds out about Khloe and they meet. With all the shit going on, you don't think she'll assume I'm messing with a bigger woman to show her not to be ashamed of her own weight? You don't think, she'll assume I'm making fun of her as well by tryna get someone big?"

"Maybe if you talk to Raina, she'll understand."

"Bro, she doesn't even talk to the therapist. How the hell am I gonna get her to open up to me?"

"Ma dukes told me she was having a hard time in therapy." I leaned my head on the seat.

"On some real shit though, I don't think continuing to sleep with Ronny is a good idea either." He said and stopped at a red light.

"Ain't that the truth. After I get dressed, I'm gonna head over there and tell her its over. I can't take the chance of Raina finding out I'm still sleeping with her after what she's been through."

"I'm not in your situation so there's no judging but I don't see how you could still do it."

"At first, I didn't wanna believe Ronny would do some shit like that and I was hoping it wasn't true. But the longer I stayed around the bitch, she started showing signs of hating fat people in general. It took me a minute to see it and while I kept her away from my daughter, I should've never stayed fucking with her. I do have love for her but after everything, it's time to leave her alone."

"You don't think Raina knows?"

"Not in the beginning but she probably figured it out." I opened the door when he parked in front of my house.

"Hit me up when you break it off with the looney chick."

"Aight. We can hit the bar afterwards because I'm sure, I'll need a drink after the whining and begging."

"No doubt." He pulled off and I went inside to get dressed and deal with this Ronny saga.

Khloe

It's my fault for allowing him back in my life. That's what I continued telling myself as I replayed his words in my head over and over.

You know I don't fuck fat bitches. I came downstairs after feeling him get up and my mom pointed to the door. I went to open it and heard part of their conversation. When those words came out his mouth, it was as if the air left my body. How could he say those things about me, or better yet, why?

The audacity of him pulling me out the club and threatening to kill me and any man who beds me. Yet; his stalker ass ex-girlfriend or whatever she is to him, shows up at my house. How in the hell did the trick even know where I lived? At this point it doesn't really matter because we are definitely finished.

I often wonder if God hated me. I mean he had to in order to send a fine man like Ryan in my life, only to have him make me fall in love and toss me away like trash. Then

Veronica calls me every name in the book, any time she sees me. Not to mention her calling and claiming to have a few of my things from Ryan's house. I only stayed there a few times and don't remember leaving anything. I told her to toss all of it but she said it's probably things I'd want.

I parked in front of some condo, checked to make sure it was the right address and stepped out. I looked around and it seemed to be a nice area. I picked my ringing phone up and it was Luna asking where I was. When I told her, she told me to leave but it was too late. The door was opened and my eyes were watering.

"Shit Risky. You feel so good." I stood there in shock as this bitch was riding him on her couch. I tried to back out quietly but my hands were shaken and the phone fell.

"Yo, What the fuck?" He stared in my eyes and sadness overtook his demeanor.

"Khloe?" The tears cascaded down my face and my anger was building.

"Why are you in my fucking house? Risky, did you tell her where I lived?"

"Hell no. K, what are you doing here?" He threw her off his lap, stood up and there was no condom. All my lunch was now over her floor.

"K?" He held my hair and rubbed my back. I pushed him away and ran out the house.

"I'm so fucking done."

"Khloe, you're done with what? Huh? Risky said he won't ever fuck a fat bitch and as you can see, we're tryna have a baby." I heard her yelling. My head snapped and his did the same to look at her.

"What the fuck you talking about Ronny? I just got here, you attacked me at the door and I was pushing your ass off because I didn't have a condom. I fucked up letting you even get that far." I felt a little better but he should've never put himself in the situation.

"Risky why are you playing me out in front of her?" This bitch had the nerve to ask and yes I did smirk.

"Oh you don't like the felling huh? Just imagine it happening all the time." I opened the car door.

"K, let me talk to you." I looked up at him and hated my heart for loving him.

"No need."

"Why did you come here?" I chuckled because listening to her, I walked in on bullshit.

"She called and said I left things at your house and she had it here. Me, not knowing, came anyway. She did this on purpose and I fell right into her trap."

"Khloe, I came to tell her it was over for good. She jumped on me and it just happened." I couldn't be mad because we weren't a couple but it still hurt to see the man you love, screwing someone else.

"Ryan, can I ask you something?" He wiped the tears off my face.

"Do you hate me?"

"Hell no. Why would I hate you?"

"I mean it's the only reason I can come up with as to why you're treating me like shit." He placed both hands on the side of my face.

"I could never hate you. I'm in.-" He couldn't finish because this hating ass bitch came over and showed me a text message. It read that he still loved her. It didn't mean that him coming to break things off weren't true but it is suspicious as hell. I checked the date and it was yesterday, which is when she called me. I wonder if she knew he was about to leave her.

"All this was a set up?" I pointed to both of them.

"Don't nobody need to set you up. I ain't know she called you."

"Yea right." He moved me away from the car so I wouldn't get in.

"The way I see it is, you both did this on purpose so I would leave you alone."

"It's about time you get it. Honey, he only wanted to know what it was like to fuck a.-" I punched her in the mouth and kept hitting her.

"That's enough K." He pulled me off and I fell on the curb.

"Ahhhhhh." I yelled out and saw how fast he turned to look at me.

184

"Shit, you ok?" He helped me up.

"I'm fine. Get off me." I got in my car and sped out the parking lot. My left foot was in extreme pain. At the light, I glanced down and couldn't see anything due to my sneaker but it felt swollen. Instead of going home, I called Luna and had her meet me at the ER.

****

"Ok, you have a fractured ankle and your big toe is broken. Right now, I'm placing your foot in a boot, which will help with the fracture and keep the toe in place to heal as well. Here is a list of orthopedic doctors too. You'll need to follow up with one in a few days." I nodded as he spoke.

"Also, you requested a blood test to check for STD's due to your partner being promiscuous and all those tests are negative. I'm going to give you a shot of penicillin just in case its too early to tell. You can follow up with your GYN. Do you have any questions?"

"No and thank you." Luna gave me a crazy look. I told her some of what happened but Ryan sexing his woman without a condom was left out. Bad enough I had to see the on-call gynecologist and go through the entire Pap smear process before she even took the blood. That was embarrassing enough.

"Hi Ms. Banks, these are your discharge papers and the medication. The doctor called it into your pharmacy if you wanna pick it up." The nurse had me sign and handed the forms to me.

"Thank you." Luna passed me the crutches, grabbed my things and walked along side of me.

"One of the guards drove your truck to the house." She told me and pulled her car around.

"I'm not gonna ask why you even thought to believe anything the chick said but I get it."
I rested my head on the seat and closed my eyes.

"We here." I opened the door and sucked my teeth after seeing the persons car in the driveway.

"What the hell happened to you?" My ignorant ass mother asked.

"I fell and fracture my ankle.

"Mmmm hmmm. Probably following behind that nigga." I can't say enough, how much I hated her coming by. I

186

needed a moment to myself and as usual, she's here to make sure I didn't have one.

"Oh like you're doing the man who left you?" Luna couldn't hold it in.

"When are you getting married? Aren't they deporting your ass outta here, right after?"

"Nope. We're gonna move right next door to you, so I can fuck with your old, hateful, using your daughter for her money, freeloading ass. And I wish you would knock on my door for some sugar." I tried not to laugh but it was hard.

"I wouldn't ask to borrow tissue from you."

"Good because I'd take a shit, wipe my ass and give that to you."

"Bitch." My mom had a way with words, I tell ya.

"Bitch. You got me fucked up." Luna started taking her earrings off.

"Ok. That's enough Luna. Help me grab my things." She stood in my mom's face ready to fight and even though my mom deserved for Luna to whoop her ass, I couldn't let it go down like that.

187

"Where you going?"

"Ma, I'm grown." I was staying at my dad's place because it's peaceful and I don't need to hear her complaining or talking shit.

"I hope you not staying with that no-good nigga who came here twenty minutes ago."

"Who?" Me and Luna asked at the same time.

"The one who said he don't fuck with fat bitches." It was funny how he wanted to be with me behind closed doors but couldn't fathom up enough strength to do it out in the open.

"He said that?" Luna asked and snapped her neck to look at me. Again, I never filled her in on everything. Some stuff I was embarrassed over and wanted to keep it to myself. *So much for that.*

"I don't wanna talk about it."

"Exactly. And you talk about me using her when that nigga clearly doing the same with sex." She sucked her teeth and walked out.

I sat on the bed and busted out crying. I was crying for tryna make a man love me who's embarrassed by my weight. I cried for the pain in my heart I had for him and the pain in my

foot. My life was in shambles right now but at least I had my

best friend and my dad.

"What the hell is going on with you Risky?" I slammed the door when he came in from helping the fat bitch off the ground.

"Let me ask you a question." He grabbed his keys and phone. I walked in the kitchen to get some ice for this black and blue eye, I was bound to have.

"What?"

"Why would you invite her over here?" He had his arms folded as he stared down at me.

"I didn't. Shit, I asked you how she found out where I lived." I could tell he was tryna figure out if I were telling the truth or not. When I called the bitch, it was from a different number and I wouldn't send her a text, for this reason right here. He can't trace anything to me and that's how its gonna stay.

"Why did she say you called her?"

"Risky, the bitch is crazy." I felt his hand on my throat so fast, I couldn't stop him. My legs were lifted off the ground

190

and I was now looking down at him because of how high he had me.

"Don't let me hear you call her a bitch, fat or anything else derogatory. Do I make myself clear?" The hate on his face and anger in his voice had me terrified. I know how he gets down in the streets and not once has he ever put his hands on me. And why is he doing it over her? I nodded my head and he let go making me fall to the ground.

"You're putting hands on me over her?" He stopped at the door and turned around.

"Your mouth is reckless."

"Risky, you have never laid hands on me."

"Listen Ronny. I came to tell you we are officially done. Don't call me for shit and I mean it." He slammed the door and I walked to the window and stared at him get in the truck. He picked his phone up and after a few seconds, I watched him toss it in the passenger side. Was he tryna call her? Matter of fact, is he in love with her?

****

"So you're telling me he choked you over the fat girl?"

Dora said as we sat in her living room using the white girl. I've become addicted to using it ever since Risky broke up with me. Yea, I used it occasionally but it became more frequent after the split.

"Yup and I don't even know why when he claims not to have any dealings with her." I nodded my head, leaned down to sniff and laid back on the couch and waited for the effects of the drug to kick in.

"Crazy right?" I said and closed my eyes.

"I'm about to take a shower. I'll be back." I never responded and balled up on the couch. Whenever I got high it would put me straight to sleep.

"What up yo?" My eyes popped open when Lamar sat next to me. I didn't care for him at all and he knew it.

His sister was the love of Risky's life and his niece was a pain in my ass. I wish the bitch would die already and I'm sure its coming. I had my little cousins who go to school with her, bullying the fuck outta her. Maybe she'll commit suicide and leave me and Risky to have our own space and more kids.

I do love her but in a different way and since she's not giving into my demands, then she can die for all I care.

"Nothing." I started to grab my things and felt him push me down on the couch.

"Move Lamar." I wasn't gonna try and fight him because he's a big, black and ugly nigga. You know the kind of man no one gives the time of day at the club but you let him buy you a drink? That's him.

"Let me taste it."

"Bye Lamar." I stood up and he kissed the side of my neck. I'm not sure if the drug had me horny or what, but it felt good.

"Yea, you like that shit." His hands went in my jeans and circled my pearl.

"Lamar, you go with Dora. Oh shitttttt." My legs got weak as he continued and brought me to a release.

"She knows I wanna fuck you. I asked her for a threesome before. Damn, that pussy taste good." His fingers were in his mouth.

"Lamar I'm not… Oh my God." He carried me in one of the rooms and locked the door. He rushed to take my clothes off and I should've been saying no but once I saw his big ass dick, I couldn't wait to feel him.

"Ssssss." His mouth was on my pussy and he munched away. I had to use the pillow to cover my mouth. After giving me three orgasms, he stood and forced himself in.

"Mmmmmm. You feel good Lamar, shit." We stayed in the room for a very long time. By the time we came out, no one was there. I asked where Dora was and he told her to go pick his niece up from his moms' house. She lived almost an hour away from what Dora told me before.

"That pussy good. No wonder that nigga stayed with you so long." I stopped washing my pussy and looked at him.

"What does that mean?"

"It means, he was ready to leave you a long time ago."

"Oh really." I had to question him because Risky didn't even fuck with him like that so how would he know?

"Yup. But I'll fuck you any day of the week."

"If you do me a favor, I may be able to make that happen." He licked his lips.

"What's that?" Him and I sat down and discussed this plan I came up with and I couldn't wait for it to take place.

"Hey uncle La.-" His niece stopped dead in her tracks when she saw me. This is the first time we've seen one another since her father told me it was over. Now that I see her, I can truly see I missed her.

"Where you come from Ronny? Lamar said you left earlier." Him and I looked at one another and he smirked. This nigga had fucking me planned. Oh well. The dick was good anyway.

"I came back to see if you wanted to go out."

"I usually stay and kick it with Raina and Lamar."

"Raina, you don't miss me." I gave her a hug and she didn't return one. I asked those two if they could give us a minute. Raina had pleading eyes for her uncle but all he was worried about is having sex again. I saw the way he licked his lips and started feeling all over Dora. The nigga didn't even wash our sex smell off and he's about to go fuck her.

195

"We'll be upstairs." Dora was giggling like a school girl. She was only with Lamar for his money because her heart is still with Waleed. Unfortunately, he didn't want her and settled for the next best thing.

"Why are you acting like that Raina?" I stood and moved over to her.

"My daddy said, I can't be around you."

"Why is that?" I snatched the McDonalds out her hand.

"Because."

"Because what?' She tried to walk away and I snatched her back.

"Because he doesn't want me sick."

"Hold up. You told your father?"

"No my nana did."

"I see. Did she tell him everything?" She put her head down, which let me know she never told our secret. If she did, I can guarantee I'd be dead already.

"Raina what did I tell you about eating all this fatty food?" I held the bag up.

"Do you want your dad to take you out the house? He won't if you're fat and disgusting."

"I'M NOT FAT! I'M NOT FAT!" She covered her ears and kept saying it while I laughed and drug her to the bathroom. I closed the door.

"Throw that shit up, right now?" She started crying and shook her head no.

"Remember what happened the last time." If she didn't listen, she had to suffer another way. I refused to place my finger in her mouth and she bite it, therefore, I came up with another way to satisfy my need.

"Please don't." She backed in the corner and tried to scream. I covered her mouth and made her remove her pants.

"Please don't do this. My daddy won't be happy." I pinched her little ass nipples because she hated it.

"Too bad he's not here. Turn around." She did what I said and I pushed her down to her knees. I unbuttoned my jeans, pulled them and my panties down and waited.

"NO!"

"Yes."

197

"Please don't make me." Her tears did nothing but turn me on. The control I had over her always gave me more pleasure. I snatched her head and placed it on my pussy." I made her lick me so good, I came hard. When she finished, I stood her up and returned the favor. I don't know why but she tasted sweet in my mouth.

"It felt good, didn't it?" She didn't say anything and pulled her clothes up.

"Didn't it?" I yanked her head.

"Yes. Can I go now?"

"Yup and if you ever mention this to anyone, I'll make sure to kill your dad and nana. Don't think because he's crazy in the streets that I can't get him and you know your grandmother can't fuck with me." I stuck my hand in her pants and pushed my finger deep inside.

"Ahhhhh." She screamed out and I covered her mouth again. If Lamar knew what I was doing to his niece, he'd kill me on the spot too.

"Are we clear?" She nodded and let the tears fall.

"You are one sexy little girl." I tongue kissed her and opened the bathroom door.

"I hate you." I heard her mumble on the way out.

"But you love the way I eat that pussy." I winked and closed the door.

Its been a long time since she let me taste her. Before anyone starts talking shit, she'll be ok. My aunt did that to me for years and I turned out fine. It's the reason, I was tryna making her skinny. I don't want a fat girlfriend. Some may think I hate her but that's not the case. The truth is, I'm going to fuck her and her dad in the future.

I walked up the stairs to Dora's room and heard her moaning. I opened the door and she was riding Lamar, who had his eyes closed at first. Once he saw me, he sat up, pulled her closer and licked his lips watching me rub on my chest. I would've done more had my phone not vibrated in my pocket. I backed away and answered it.

"WHAT?"

"Veronica are you ok? I haven't seen you here in weeks." My psychiatrist asked. I've been seeing her for years.

"I'll be there in an hour. My medication ran out."

"Good. I'll see you soon." I hung up and went downstairs to grab my things. Raina was on the couch crying. I thought about making her do me again since watching Lamar turned me on but I really needed to get some new medicine. My shit ran out two days ago.

****

"How have you been Veronica?" The doctor asked and stared at me from the chair.

"I'm good. Can I have my medicine?"

"Did you hurt anyone?" I sucked my teeth.

"No. Can I have it now?"

"Veronica, are you sure because I don't want you to do to someone else, what was done to you." I laid my head back and closed my eyes.

"I feel bad for doing it but when she's around, I can't help myself. She's so sexy to me and let's not mention, how good she tastes."

"Who are you talking about?"

"My girlfriend."

"Oh, I didn't know you and Ryan broke up." I turned around and saw her writing stuff on her notepad.

"Yea, he still fucks me though."

"Veronica, how old is the woman?" She was looking at me with her glasses on the bridge of her nose.

"What woman?"

"The woman you love." I sat up.

"Who said I loved her?" Was I really in love with a child?

"How old is she?"

"Twelve."

"What's her name?"

"If I tell you, you'll take her away from me and I can't have that." I stood up and grabbed my things.

"This is my last meeting." The doctor stood up.

"Veronica, what you're doing is not love. You are molesting that child. Please tell me who she is so I can get her help."

"NO! THEN YOU'LL TAKE HER AWAY, LIKE YOU TOOK THE OTHER ONE."

"What other one? Oh God, please don't tell me there were more." I laughed and snatched the prescription off her desk. How stupid was she to have it written out already?

"CALL THE COPS. VERONICA! VERONICA!" I heard her screaming as I ran out the door. Fuck that. She's not taking Raina from me and neither is her father. I don't know why she's calling the cops because they'll never find me and they can't prove anything if they did.

Luna

"Still plump huh?" I rolled my eyes at Oscar. He was supposed to be here last week but cancelled for some reason. It didn't matter to me because I had yet to inform Waleed of this fake ass marriage. Plus, he went outta town, which makes it better because I didn't have to hide. We may not have a title but everyone knew I belonged to Waleed.

"Is that why you're here? To see if I'm still fat."

"I said plump, not fat."

"What's the difference?" We hugged and he sat across from me in this expensive ass spot. Instead of meeting in Jersey, we were in New York at some overpriced restaurant.

"The difference is, fat is much bigger than you and plump means, you're definitely not skinny and on your way to being fat. Which brings me to why I'm here." I had to hold my composure or I would smack the fuck outta him.

"I need you in the gym everyday for at least two hours. Your diet will be changed and you need to stop fucking that nigga." I looked up at him and there was a photo in his phone of Waleed and I, sitting on one of the benches at the boardwalk. I remembered the day because he told me it was corny, yet by the end of the night he said, it was peaceful and he would do it again.

"Do I tell you to rid yourself of all the bitches you're sleeping with?" He chuckled.

"It's a difference baby and you know it." He snapped his fingers for a waitress and she came right over.

"If you wanna continue with him be my guest but how's he gonna feel in a couple of months when you move to Mexico and leave him hanging?"

"Who the hell said anything about moving there?"

"It's in the agreement love." He took a piece of paper out and scooted it over to me. I glanced over it and couldn't believe my eyes.

Inside the document it stated, we are to be married in a few months and underneath in the fine print were stipulations. I had to be 140 pounds or less. I must produce four kids within the next four years. I have to allow him to satisfy his sexual appetite with me and whomever he chooses. I also have to partake in some business ventures as well as, attending meetings and making sure the men involved are satisfied. Basically, making me a prostitute wife.

"When was this contract made because one... I don't remember these stipulations being in it and two... I'm not about to fuck men to get their business. What the hell is wrong with you?"

"Aren't you sleeping with the dude for your father?"

"Say what?" To my knowledge neither of them knew one another. I had no clue what he was talking about.

"Your pops is tryna get him to cop from us before I take over."

"I?"

"I mean, we." He gave me a fake smile.

"The dude he fucks with now out in Puerto Rico gives him a good deal and I told your pops, he'll have to match it or drop his prices. I guess he thought you sleeping with him would steer him in his direction. So when I take over." He caught himself.

"I mean we take over, it'll be even more money coming in." Not only was I pissed about the contract but how the hell did my father know about Waleed? I know he's had people watching me and most likely did a background check but if Oscar's saying all this, my dad has been plotting for a while.

We ordered our food and ate in silence. He and I were both in deep thought and probably over different things. The only thing on my mind was the shit my dad knew and planning. After we said our goodbyes, I drove straight to my parents' house and stormed inside. They were on the couch watching television.

"Hola, mamacita." My mom said and turned to finish watching TV.

"When were you gonna tell me, I had to solicit my body at business meetings?" My mom turned the TV down and looked at my father.

"What are you talking about?"

"Don't act like you don't know. This is your fucking signature isn't it?" I tossed the paper at him.

WHAP! WHAP! He slapped the shit outta me. My mom covered her mouth because he's never laid hands on me.

"Let me tell you something little girl." He had me against the wall.

"I have no idea what you're talking about but if you ever disrespect me like that again, I'll knock your head off. Do you hear me?" I shook my head yes and let the tears fall. He snatched the paper off the ground and both him and my mom scanned it.

"If you had asked me, I would've told you this isn't my signature. It resembles it but this is not mine. And for you to even think I'd let you prostitute yourself tells me you have no faith or trust in me."

"Daddy."

"No Luna. I know you don't like the arrangement but it's what's best for everyone but never in my life would I have signed this." He walked out and slammed the door to his office.

"Oh Mija! I know your dad goes overboard sometimes but to accuse him of something so degrading is showing whoever did this, we aren't one. Did you show anger or disgust when you received this from Oscar?" She knew it came from

him because I told her we were meeting up tonight.

"Yes." I put my head down.

"Honey, your father just told me tonight that something

wasn't right with him, which is why he sent four truckloads of

people to follow you."

"But why?"

"I'm not sure but as the wedding approaches he's been

moving funny. For example, why is he here? He's only come

to the states maybe four times since he was a kid. Nothing that

he does requires him to step foot over here."

"But he said daddy is tryna get me to woo Waleed so he

could purchase drugs from him."

"Who?" My dad came from out his office.

"Waleed."

"I don't know no damn Waheed or Wakeed."

"It's Waleed daddy and he's the guy I've been seeing."

"Oh Wale."

"Wale?"

"That's what the streets call him for short." I wonder why he never told me to call him that.

"Yea I've seen him around you and of course his name rings bells in the streets but I don't need any new people on a team I'm about to hand over. That would be stupid."

"Why is that?" I was offended he didn't wanna work with my man.

"If I'm giving everything up in a few months. When would I have the time to feel this guy out? Why would I take the time to do it? Putting new people on a team requires putting them through a serious of tests, running extensive background checks, finding each and every one of their family members and the list goes on and on. Anyone you and Oscar want on your team will be strictly because you chose them."

"But I don't want this daddy. Why didn't you give it to your other daughter?"

WHAP! WHAP! And just like that he smacked me again and this time my mom jumped in the middle.

"CARLOS, I SWEAR BEFORE GOD IF YOU HIT MY CHILD AGAIN."

"She knows better than to mention that devil in this house."

It's true, I did know better. My dad cheated on my mom when I was around five years old and the woman kept the child, to spite my mom. You know the side chick who won't get rid of the child, thinking it will make the man come to her. Anyway, my dad wanted nothing to do with the child because my mother left him. It took her two years to take him back and when she did, my mom accepted the child with open arms. Little did we know; her mom made an attempt on my mom's life quite a few times and my dad terminated her.

Long story short, my mom made my father bring my sister here. On her 18th birthday, she tried to kill my mom and I walked in on her. My mom had stab wounds all over her body. Had I not gotten there in time, she would've drowned in her own blood. Later on that night, I found the bitch and both me and Khloe whooped her ass so bad she was in ICU for weeks. My mom begged my dad not to kill her because she was probably trying to retaliate for her mom.

The one time I did try and kill her, my father stopped me right before I pulled the trigger. He said, my mother would never forgive me and he was right. Once she found out, she cursed me out for two days but I didn't care. Which is why every time I see my sister, I beat her ass. I didn't this last time because we were in a club and celebrating Khloe's promotion but I'm sure the time is coming for me to do it again.

"She's the one who wants to be rich. You tossed her out with nothing. Give it to her." I snatched my things and went towards the door.

"Oh mom, make sure you watch your back. Your husbands love child is in town wishing death on me. But don't you worry. I got it covered." I slammed the door and walked to my car. I was pissed and went straight to the place I frequented a lot but stopped when Waleed started taking up my time.

"Ms. Suarez, long time no see."

"Whatever Rico. I got a thousand on me right now. If I need more you know I'm good for it." He smiled and let his tongue glide over his teeth. He's been tryna fuck me for years.

"Let's go." He grabbed my hand and led the way.

211

"Long time no see." The gentlemen said and offered me a seat. Lord knows I needed this to relax my mind.

Waleed

"What up chunky?" I smiled because she hated me calling her that but I loved it.

"Anyway, I wanted to discuss something with you."

"Shoot." I was standing outside rolling dice.

"Ummmm."

"Why you sound nervous? You fucked someone?"

"Waleed." When she ignored the question, I threw the dice and moved out of ear range from these nosy niggas.

"Did you sleep with someone else?" She tried to speak and I cut her off.

"I'm out yo."

"WALEED!" I heard her scream and disconnected the call.

"I'll see y'all tomorrow." I dapped them up and hopped in my car. Was I pissed! Hell yea. Here I am being a faithful nigga and she throwing the pussy out to whoever catches it. I mean we don't have a title and I can't say she's cheating but damn. I'm running up in her shit raw any chance I get.

I stopped at the liquor store, picked up two bottles of Henny and some blunts. Ima need to relax before I go see Luna because right now, killing her is the only thing on my mind. I also had to keep in mind she never said she slept with someone else. I cut her off but it doesn't mean she didn't. What other reason would she have for hesitating and saying we need to talk?

I parked in front of my house, pressed the gate and drove in. I never worried about anyone coming here and only had the gate because my mom stayed here a lot and said it made her feel safe, when I'm away. I wonder how she'll take it when she hears about Luna. My mom loved her and she could do no wrong in my mom's eyes. But this bitch here. My mom couldn't stand and would probably beat her ass if she were here. I shut the car off, opened the door and shook my head. How did this bitch know where I lived? She obviously waited for me to open the gate in order to be this close.

"Not tonight Julie and how you know where I live?"

"Why you treating me like this?" I raised my eyebrow at her. I discussed this with her already the last time we ran into one another.

"Bye." I closed the door, went upstairs to shower and five minutes later, this bitch stepped in. She was on some fatal attraction type shit.

"What you doing?" Julie kneeled down and literally swallowed me whole. I mean she gobbled my dick up just like old times. I came and pulled outta her mouth.

"You can go now."

"I don't think you really want that." She lifted her leg and started playing with herself. My dick woke right up. I shut the water off, carried her in the room, took some condoms out my drawer and slid right in.

"Mmmmm. Just like I remember." She moaned out and wrapped her legs around my back.

"Let me get on top." I laid on my back and watched her mount me. My hands went on her waist and for a moment, I swore she had a smirk on her face looking to the door. I stopped her, turned my head and no one was there.

"Wale, you feel so good." No one called me Waleed except Luna. I stared at Julie about to cum and it was something familiar but I couldn't put my finger on it.

"Shit, I'm cumming." I felt my nut coming and removed her off my dick. I stood and flushed the condom down the toilet. I stared at myself in the mirror and felt like shit for sleeping with someone else.

****

"Man, I messed around and slept with Julie." Risky shook his head

"More than once." I said, disappointed in myself.

"What's more than once? More than one time in a day, or a few days in a row."

"Maybe four times over the last week on different days and a whole lot within those days."

"What am I missing? I thought you said Luna was the one."

"She is. Well she was." I started telling him what happened and he said I should've waited. I agree but oh well.

"Have you spoken to Luna?"

216

"Nah. I tried to call and she changed her phone number and she's never home when I stopped by. She's probably mad I hung up on her the night she tried to tell me. Then I had a ton of missed calls and text messages from her but I never responded. Its not like I could anyway because I was fucking Julie."

"Damn."

"I know right."

PHEW! PHEW! The two bodies dropped in front of us. I removed my gloves and threw it and the gun down the incinerator.

"What you about to do now?" He asked and waited for me to leave.

"Go try and see her." I slapped hands with him and hopped in my car. On the drive over, all I thought about is Luna giving her body to someone else. I pressed the button on her gate and she answered.

"Let me in babe."

"For what?" I could picture her chunky ass standing there with her arms folded.

217

"So I can dick you down and shift your uterus. And why your number changed?"

"Waleed, I thought we had something."

"What you talking about?"

"Whatever we had is over. I don't want anything to do with you." I heard her sniffling.

"Yo, what's really good? You know I don't play these games."

"I guess you needed to know what it's like to sleep with a fat girl too huh?"

"Luna, I've never called you that. Yo, come out here. I don't wanna talk through this stupid intercom."

"I hate you Waleed. I hate you for making me fall in love with you and I hate you for making me believe what we had was real."

"Yo, are you serious?" I cut my car off and walked around the gate to see if I could jump it. I needed to see what the hell is going on. I pressed the button over and over.

"If you jump the gate, someone will shoot you on the spot. If you don't believe me look on my roof." I did and sure enough there were at least three dudes standing there with long rifles.

"This what you want Luna?"

"This is what you wanted Wale." *What the fuck did she just call me?* She's never called me anything but Waleed. No one even called me Wale in front of her. Did she know about Julie? Nah. I don't see her holding that in. But she did call me Wale over the intercom. Nah. I shook my head and walked to my car. I don't know what's going on and right now I'm not even tryna figure it out. I pulled out and took my ass home. Whatever it is, I'm sure she'll tell me eventually because she's never been one to bite her tongue.

Risky

"Raina, this session and any future ones won't work if you only sit here." The psychiatrist told my daughter, who was sitting close to me on the couch.

Ever since my mom informed me of the shit Ronny had her doing, she completely shut down. Then, she met some lady at Red Lobster and my mom said she opened up to her. Now they speak on the phone but I have yet to meet or speak to her. She usually meets them at the mall or movies. My mom said it's too loosen her up to talk.

It's definitely working because Raina was back to being her normal self. She started talking to us more and even asked to go out with me. I wasn't ashamed of her and had no problem taking her wherever she wanted to go. It's just, I couldn't get her to leave the house unless it was school. And even then, one of us had to be right there when the bell rang. The shit bothered the hell outta me but the doctor said we had to be patient.

"Is the session over yet?" Raina looked up at me.

"Raina, I know it's embarrassing to talk about but they're a lot of kids who've been in the same situation."

"I'll be fine talking to Ms. K and she's free daddy. You don't have to pay her to watch me sit." She rolled her eyes at the doctor.

"Who is Ms. K?" The doctor asked and Raina's face lit up.

"I met her one day in the bathroom and she was really nice. I talk to her a lot."

"Is she a doctor?"

"No but she's been through this before too. Well not everything."

"What's everything?" And just like that she shut down.

"Raina, is something else happening?" She broke down crying hysterical. Whatever it was had her shaking and it only angered me more. I had to meet this woman and ask her to find out from my daughter what else is going on. Its clear she's not opening up for us so if she can do it, I'm all for it.

"Ok let's end the session." She handed Raina a tissue.

"Can I speak to you outside?" I stood and followed her out the door.

"Two things." We moved away so Raina couldn't hear.

"One... we need to get this Ms. K in here. She seems to like talking to her and appears to be getting more information than us."

"And two..." I asked and waited for her to answer. She looked uncomfortable at the moment.

"I think someone is touching her."

"SAY WHAT?" I started towards the door. She grabbed me back.

"Mr. Wells, I understand your concern but if you go in there upset like this, she's not gonna answer you."

"I need to find the person."

"I know but we need to be sure and the only person she's speaking to is Ms. K. We need her in here ASAP. Matter of fact, go in Raina's phone and send her a message to meet her here Friday, for our session. That way we can both meet her. Make sure you put an earlier time so I can speak to her first. I mean, if you're ok with that." I was pacing back and forth.

"Why do you think she's being touched?"

"She is showing the signs. For example, Raina is started to eat a lot more right?" I nodded.

"You said she seems depressed and I can see the anxiety on her face every time we meet. She's told me about nightmares and thoughts of suicide." The more she spoke, the angrier I became.

"Fuck! Now what?" People were staring at me because of how loud I was but I didn't care.

"I think we definitely need to meet with this woman and hopefully she can help us. Let's go tell Raina we'll meet on Friday and have Ms. K surprise her. If she's comfortable with her, she'll open up." I nodded and picked my phone up to call my mother.

"OH MY GODD! CALL 911!" She shouted and I ran in the office to find my daughter lying on the ground with slits to her wrists and something sticking out her neck. What the fuck happened in those few minutes? I tried to lift her but the doctor wouldn't let me.

"NOOOOO! We don't know how far it went in. You don't wanna take the chance of her bleeding out." She grabbed some paper towels and told me to put them on her wrists and apply pressure. I watched her trying to figure out a way to keep the blood from leaking out.

"What the fuck is that?" I gestured with my eyes to the thing poking out Raina's neck.

"A letter opener. It was on my desk and she must've saw it. I'm sorry. Shittttt. Where is the ambulance?" A few seconds later, the paramedics rushed in and told both of us to move. They wrapped gauze around Raina's wrist and neck. I could no longer hold back my tears and let them fall as I followed them out and into the ambulance.

"Call her." The doctor threw me Raina's phone before they closed the door. I stared at the people working on my daughter. She had an IV bag being placed on her arm and monitors on her chest.

"Get to the hospital." I told my mom and called Waleed and relayed the same message. Neither of them asked questions and hung up.

When the paramedics pulled up, I jumped out first. They lifted the stretcher and rushed her inside. Doctors and nurses ran over and took her in the back. My heart was racing and all I could think of is her dying. I have no idea how long I was standing there and tears were pouring down my face so bad, I didn't notice Waleed or my mom come in.

"Raina, tried to kill herself. Well, I don't know if she did. It was a lotta blood and.-" I couldn't even get the words out.

"Oh my God!" My mom hugged me and then walked out and picked her phone up to call someone. Probably the damn pastor of the fake church she goes to.

"She's gonna make it bro. My niece ain't going out like that." The therapist came running through the doors.

"Fuck! I need to call Lamar." Waleed sucked how teeth.

"She's his niece too and he loves her." He took my phone and called him. I put my head against the wall and prayed to God my daughter was ok. About fifteen minutes later, she came in limping. She was still beautiful as ever to me and I had a lotta making up to do if I wanted her in my life.

"Where is she? Is she ok?" She went straight to my mother and gave her a hug. Waleed looked at me.

"What are you doing here?" I questioned and she turned around.

"I'm here for Raina. Why are you here? Are you ok?" I smiled because she was concerned. Then I put two and two together. This must be Ms. K.

"Raina is my daughter." The shocked looked on her face told me she had no idea. It really is a small fucking world.

Khloe

"Are you serious?" I asked Ryan who informed me Raina is his daughter.

"Very serious."

"I'm so sorry. Do you know what happened?"

"I was there." I covered my mouth.

"I don't wanna talk about it right now. Once the doctor tells me she's ok, I can tell you." I nodded and sat down. I took a seat next to him and he put my foot on his lap. I gave him a weird look. Here we are in public and he's actually catering to me.

"How's your foot?" The boot was still on from the day I fell at his ex-girlfriend's house.

"I still have a lotta pain in it but I'll be fine." He let his head rest against the wall and stared at the ceiling.

I was talking to his mom and noticed worry on his face. How did I not know he was her dad? It's not like he wasn't active in Raina's life because she adored him. It was always daddy this, daddy that. It never dawned on me to ask his name.

I stood to use the bathroom and when I came out he was standing there crying.

"She's gonna be ok Ryan." I wrapped my arms around him and he cried harder.

"You didn't see her K. She had blood draining from her wrists and the thing in her neck was deep."

"Come in here." I pulled him in the bathroom with me. When I closed the door, I grabbed a paper towel to wipe his face and he was behind me staring in the mirror.

"K."

"Not right now." I didn't wanna discuss anything between us.

"I don't know what I'll do if..." I put my index finger on his lips.

"Don't even speak it into existence." Once he gathered himself, I opened the door and I was ready to fight.

"I swear, I'm gonna beat her ass if she says one word to me." I told him and once he peeked out, anger over took his body. He ran up on Veronica and knocked her out. Her head hit the ground and he started kicking her in the side.

"Yoooooo. That's enough bro." Waleed and another guy had to pull him off and take him outside. His mom was crying and the other woman Veronica is always with, was crying too.

"Look, I know it's been a minute but can you talk to him?" Waleed asked as he came in with an evil look on his face. I wasn't sure why he was asking me but I went ahead and limped out behind him.

"What the fuck?" Ryan was now beating the crap out the dude. Outta nowhere he placed a gun on the guys forehead.

"RYAN NO!" He looked up.

"He blames me K." I limped over to him.

"Baby don't do this. Raina is gonna wake up and look for you. Please don't do this." I felt his arm lowering. He hit the guy a few more times with the butt of his gun and blood was everywhere.

"Hold this." He put the safety on and slid the gun in my waist. Cops started swarming in and I began to panic.

"I won't let anything happen to you." He wrapped his arms around me.

"Is everything ok out here?" One of the cops asked and stared down at the guy.

"Yea. You know Lamar always tryna fight."

"He knows his punk ass never wins." Him and a few cops started talking like nothing happened. After they finished and got in their cars to leave, I punched him in the chest.

"What?" He thought the shit was funny."

"I wanted to see if you were my ride or die."

"By giving me a gun?"

"At least, it doesn't have a body on it yet."

"Ughhhh. Let's go." I grabbed his hand and we stepped in just as the doctor emerged asking for her family. He pulled us in a corner and started explaining.

"Ok. Raina suffered a stab wound to her neck and deep slits to her wrists. As you know, we had to give her a blood transfusion." Ryan nodded his head.

"She required ten stitches in both wrists and her neck has seven. If she pushed a little deeper I'm afraid she wouldn't be here."

"Can I see her?" Ryan was anxious to see her and I don't blame him. I was too but I would never overstep and ask to see her before him.

"Yes but let me tell you a few things." He asked if everybody were her family and he said yes, except for the guy Lamar he beat up who just walked in. He was fucked up too. The other chick stood there looking dumb. The four of us stepped in a room and he closed the door.

"Unfortunately, your daughter is considered a threat to herself, therefore she has straps around her wrists and waist."

"What the fuck?" He instantly started snapping.

"Ryan try and calm down. Let's hear what he has to say." I held his hand.

"They're only for precaution. They will be taken off when she gets to the adolescent ward for crisis."

"Doctor speak in terms for dummies." Waleed said making us laugh.

"She's going to be put on the crazy floor for kids and child services will be involved. Raina will be required to stay for a week before she can go home. Please don't worry because the case manager will keep you updated every step of the way. No medication will be given to her, no tests can be run on her unless you give written consent." He went on and on about what to expect and took us to the spot Raina was in. She was lying there staring at the wall.

"Daddy." She tried to lift her arms. You could see her looking down and start crying. I stayed by the door with his mom and Waleed.

"Oh hell no." Ryan tried to remove the straps. I ran over, pushed his hands away and placed both of mine on his face.

"Ryan, let me talk to you." It took him a minute but he walked in the hallway with me.

"Baby, I know it looks bad."

"K, they have her looking like a..."

"A crazy person." I finished his sentence.

"She's not crazy." He sat down and I stood in front of him.

"Raina is not crazy but she needs help Ryan and this is the best place for her. You may not like it but at least no one can get to her."

"I want her home."

"I know you do. Ryan, she needs her father to understand what she's going through. Don't let her see you upset and fighting with everyone because she may blame herself. Let's go hear what the people have to say and go from there." He nodded his head and stood up.

"How do you know so much?"

"I've been in Raina's place before and trust me when I say, it's very dark and hard to come out of." He didn't say anything.

We went in the room and a woman in a suit was standing there. I told him to relax and let her speak. Once she gave us the rundown of what would happen she gave Ryan some alone time with her. Afterwards they were taking Raina upstairs to the crisis floor.

"I'm sorry daddy. I just wanted the pain to go away. I wanted the kids to stop bothering me and her too."

"Raina."

"Daddy please don't be mad."

"I'm not mad baby. Scared of losing you but not mad."
He rubbed her hair and kissed her forehead.

"All I ask is you never try this again. If you need to talk,
call Ms. K or.-"

"You know Ms. K?" He gestured for me to come over.

"Hey lil mama." I sat on the side of the bed.

"Ms. K, I tried to ignore the kids. I did and she came
around and..." she stopped herself and started crying again.

"Who came around Raina?" She looked at her dad.

"Was it daddy's girlfriend?" He pinched me on the side.

"His ex-girlfriend. Daddy she found me at uncle
Lamar's house." I turned around quickly and Waleed blocked
the door.

"Look at me Ryan. Look." He was fuming and ready to
find the Lamar guy again and most likely kill him.

"Another time. Let's make sure she gets better."

"I'm gonna kill her." We all knew he spoke of his ex. The door opened and the lady walked in with two guys who looked like techs.

"Daddy please don't let them take me." She started crying and screaming.

"Can y'all give me another minute with her please?" At first no one moved. After Ryan barked, the lady and two guys stepped out the door. I held her hand.

"Raina, I know it's scary and you want your dad to take you home." She nodded her head.

"I understand but honey this is the best place for you. The people here wanna help you and none of us want to see this happen again, so I need you to do me a favor." I wiped her eyes and asked his mom to wet a paper towel in the small sink so I can clean her face. She handed it to me.

"I need you to stay calm and do what they ask. Then, I want you to call me or your dad when they put you in a room. It will give us peace of mind that you're ok."

"But..."

"Raina she can't get you in here and I promise if she comes within one inch of you, I'm beating her ass." She smiled.

"There's the smile I'm used to seeing. I'll be here first thing in the morning to see you."

"Can you bring my dad?"

"Girl he'll probably beat me here."

"I love you uncle Leed. I love you too nana and daddy. Please don't let them make me live here."

"You won't be here longer than a week and I'm gonna try and break you out before then." I kissed her cheek and moved away so everyone else could have their moment.

"We'll see you in the morning." I let the people in and we all watched them take her out on the stretcher.

"Sir, you're under arrest for assault on Veronica Hicks." I looked at him.

"My mom has it." He had taken the gun out my waist when we went in the room with Raina.

"But how are they arresting you? I thought you were cool with the cops."

"There's always one baby. I'll see you later." The cop placed handcuffs on him and took him to the car. Today has been one hell of a day.

Luna

"Hey lil mama. How are you?" I asked Raina. Me and Khloe were at the hospital visiting her. I was gonna come last night but once she informed me that stupid ass Waleed came, I changed my mind.

See, I met Raina a while back when Khloe told me about their interaction at the Red Lobster. At first, I laughed my ass off about how the little girl tried to come for her. Then she explained the rest and we've been like adopted aunts to her. Well, Khloe is closer because they speak a lot more. Plus, she's gone through the same thing as Raina, growing up. The bullying at school and let's not discuss how her mom disrespects her on a regular.

"I'm ok. I wanna go home." She hugged both of us and stood by the window. She had two gowns on and her facial expression was sad. Khloe sat the bag of clothes down we picked up from the mall for her. They wouldn't allow us to visit until after eleven so we ran there first.

"Is my daddy coming?"

"Oh shit heffa. We not good enough?" She started laughing and sat down.

"I really appreciate you two coming but I wanna go home and he's the only one who can make it happen." Khloe took her hand in hers.

"Raina it hasn't even been a full 24 hours yet. The case manager said you won't speak during the sessions and you haven't eaten."

"We only had one session last night and another one this morning. She keeps asking me the same questions."

"And what's that?"

"You know, why did you try to kill yourself? Would you do it again? Blah, blah, blah." She rolled her eyes.

"If you're tryna get outta here, give them something." Khloe tried reasoning with her but all she wanted to do is go home.

"Yea. Tell them about the bullying at school but don't give names. Your dad would kick your ass for snitching." I said and both of them almost fell out the chair from laughing.

"Raina, I'm gonna ask you a question and I need you to be honest with me." Khloe had a serious tone. She looked around the room to make sure no one was paying attention.

"Is someone touching you?" Tears just started racing down her face. Ryan told her the therapist made the observation from Raina's behaviors and asked if she could find out for him.

"I don't want it to happen but the person keeps saying I like it. And..."

"OH HELL NO! Who the fuck is it?" Khloe jumped up and I had to calm her down.

"Please don't say anything Ms. K. The person said they'd kill my dad and nana. I already lost my mom. I can't lose them too." And just like that, both of us were upset.

"Raina you have to tell your father. He can handle it." Khloe tried reasoning with her.

"I don't want him to look at me different or think I wanted it because I never said anything."

"He would never assume that." I told her. Mannnn, adults really have mind control over kids. I'm assuming its an adult because a kid won't say no shit like that.

"Please." She was begging for her not to tell.

"I'm scared to ask but how long has it been going on?" When she told Khloe 3 years, both of us started crying.

"Please don't tell him."

"Raina how can he protect you from the person if he doesn't know who it is?" She moved next to her and Raina jumped.

"Raina, we wanna make sure this person never bothers you again but you have to give us a name or something."

"Not right now. Please let me tell my dad when I'm ready."

"I don't know Raina. This is big and…"

"Please. I don't wanna stress him out right now. I promise to tell him soon." Khloe wiped her eyes and all three of us sat there in silence for what felt like forever. I think we were all in our own thoughts, especially; Khloe. I know it was gonna be hard for her to keep this secret. It would be for me.

"Here. Luna and I brought you some clothes to wear. This gown is not poppin." She smiled and went in the bathroom.

"K, you have to tell him." She ran her hand through her hair.

"I know but then her trust will be broken with me and that's the last thing she needs."

"But what if the person comes back?"

"I haven't thought that far but I'll have something figured out before she comes home."

A few minutes later Raina walked out in a pair of jeans, a hoodie from Abercrombie she had to have the last time we took her shopping and a pair if all black Jordan's. We both loved spoiling her and she did too. K pulled a brush and ponytail holder out and started doing her hair. By the time she finished, Raina looked like nothing ever happened. There was a bandage on her neck and her wrists were covered by the hoodie but she looked good.

"DADDY!" She screamed and ran over to him, Waleed and her grandmother.

"Well damn. I guess my girl brought you clothes."

"Your girl? Daddy, you and Ms. K just met. She can't be your girl yet?" Of course, I was cracking up because they never told her their affiliation. However, Khloe smacked me in the arm and told me to worry about Waleed, who was giving me the evil eye.

"Why you look like yesterday?" Raina asked and he didn't hesitate to tell her.

"Oh, I knocked Veronica out last night and she called the cops."

"You should've killed her. I hate that bitch." She mumbled but Khloe and I heard her.

"Well now that you're here. We're gonna go." I stood and Waleed wouldn't take his eyes off me.

"Thanks for everything Khloe. You have no idea; how much I appreciate it." Risky walked over to her and she pushed him away without letting Raina see. I could tell he was wondering why. My girl didn't wanna give him any false hope of them being together. I'm not saying she's over him but she isn't fucking with him like that either.

"We'll be back tomorrow Raina and call if you need anything." She gave us a hug and we opened the door to leave.

"What's really good yo?" Waleed snatched my arm. Instead of tryna make him guess what my problem was, I gave him some clues. Yea, I was being petty because I could've told him.

"The night I told you we needed to discuss something and you hung up on me, what did you do?"

"I went to the liquor store and home. Why?"

"Hmph."

"Hmph what?"

"Were you alone?" He folded his arms and stared at me.

"All you had to do was tell me, I was too fat or not someone you could make your girl. A man like you and your friend are used to bad bitches so I get it. But if it was just a fuck, then you should've left it at that. Instead, you strung me along and made me fall and hard too. Don't you worry though. Someone is there to pick up the pieces." I blew him a kiss and he literally threw me against the wall.

"You think I'm playing with you Luna? Huh?"

"Let Go Waleed." Khloe was tryna pull his hands off my neck.

"I will chop your fucking head off and send it to your father in a box if you fuck someone else."

"Let her go man." Risky finally pulled him off and after catching my breath, I looked over at him. He was breathing heavy and making a ton of threats.

"I bet my new nigga gets way better sex treatment than I gave you." Now what type of person would I be if I didn't fuck with him?

"WHAT?" He tried to get away from Risky and now another dude, who held him back.

"Just go Luna."

"Fuck you nigga. I hope your dick falls off." I stuck my finger up, grabbed Khloe's hand and ran down the hall. I wasn't sure if he'd break free and really kill me.

I didn't feel safe until we were in my truck leaving and even then, I felt like he was watching me. *Crazy ass motherfucker!*

"Back so soon?" I asked Oscar. He looked like he saw a ghost and tried to walk away. I was in the mall looking for some shoes to go out for my birthday. Khloe and I didn't wanna go out around here so we rented a suite in New York and planned on partying all weekend long.

"What? What? Are you doing here?"

"I live here and why are you stuttering?" He picked his phone up and started texting away.

"I don't care about any of these bitches you out here screwing, so you can relax." He smirked.

"You have no idea, do you?"

"No idea about what?"

"Nothing. You'll know soon enough." He waved me off and went in the opposite direction. I don't even have the patience or tolerance to be bothered with his bullshit. I continued shopping and ended up sitting in Ruby Tuesday's at the mall. I saw the dirty Dora chick with some big black guy in a booth.

"It's not enough food here to feed you." She said. I took my open hand and with all my might SMACKED THE FUCK OUTTA HER.

"Oh shit yo." Dude started laughing as her nose gushed out blood.

"I ate it all before you got here that's why the trays are refilled, you stupid bitch." I yanked her head back.

"You stay worried about my weight when you should be worried why this man don't even have your back. Had this been a real nigga, he would've stepped to me." I let go.

"Bitch ass nigga." I said and looked him up and down. You ever see a nigga you know ain't shit? That's him right here. Who allows a chick to fight or even hit his girl and he stay seated. Woman or not, he should've said something.

"What the fuck you say?" He stood up.

"You heard me." He came closer and I did what any woman would do when a big, black, gorilla looking nigga stood in front of her. Yup, I kicked him in the nuts and once he leaned over, hit him in the face with my purse.

247

"Fuck both of y'all." I sashayed my fat ass right on out and went home. *Fuck everybody!*

Khloe

"This room is to die for?" I told Luna. Today was her birthday and she wanted to party in New York. I had no problem with it because we were away from the drama in Jersey.

"Hell yea." She came over to the window and looked down. People were everywhere and the lights made it so much prettier. People can say its not all that but when you look at the view from a certain point, its really beautiful.

"How's Raina?"

"She's good. Her and my mother got into already." Raina was released from the hospital two days ago and begged her father to stay with me. At first, he was against it because he couldn't protect her. Unfortunately, I offered him a room down the hall and he hopped right on it. So imagine all three of us in a house and my mother popping up when she wants. I give it to Raina though, she gave my mom a taste of her own medicine.

"And her pappy?" I had to smile because he was trying to talk to me and I'd go in my room or tell him he was being rude because Raina and I were talking. He'd just walk away with his head down. I still love him, hell I'm still in love with him but I can't be with a man who's ashamed of who he loves.

I admit that in the beginning, it was supposed to be about the sex but like most women, we believe the lies, fall for the bullshit and somehow get caught up in the illusion of sexy man really wanting more. I learned my lesson, that's for sure.

"Not a damn thing." I unpacked my things and placed them in one of the drawers. We were only here the weekend but I always made myself at home.

"Yea ok. One horny night and guess who's going on a Risky ride?"

"I'm not gonna lie. A bitch do miss it. The way he takes his time and makes sure I get mine a few times before him, shows how much he appreciates my body. The long talks we used to have and the getaway plans he wanted to go on, really had me believing he was my man."

"Ugh, he was."

"Yea but only behind closed doors." She nodded and I changed the subject.

"And what about that psychopath you're dealing with?" She waved me off.

"Hell no bitch. Tell me." I plopped down on the sofa and waited for Luna to give me the details of Waleed's latest craziness.

"Nothing much."

"Ugh, what's nothing much because you'll say that and it really be a lot more to it." I told her.

"He keeps threatening to end my life if I sleep with someone else. You know, the normal that he's been doing. Oh and he's gonna knock my teeth out regardless for having a slick mouth and to make sure no man gets their dick sucked again." My stomach was hurting from laughing so hard. Those two are pure comedy and I always get a kick outta them. She sat next to me and laid her head on my shoulder.

"Do you know if we weren't big girls, we'd have the perfect men? Fine, rich and great in bed." She said and I had to agree.

"I know." I rested my head on the couch.

"You ever thought about going on a diet?" I asked and she looked at me.

"For the sake of love, I've thought about it. But then, I had to think about my own happiness."

"What you mean?" She made herself comfortable before answering.

"I'd be asking myself everyday if it's worth it. I mean we could lose weight, be the baddest bitches walking the planet and a nigga still cheat. Trump did it to his wife." I almost fell out of the couch from laughing at that crazy ass analogy.

"Bitch his wife ain't bad. She looks like a damn orange; plastic Barbie and I'm not talking the original Barbie. I'm talking about the ones in the dollar store. The low budget ones." She busted out laughing.

"But seriously, after hearing Risky tell that heffa he didn't sleep with fat girls I contemplated going back to my old ways." She looked at me.

I used to eat just to throw up and I fucked up my stomach lining really bad. Everything Raina was going through, I've been there and done that, which is why I can relate so well.

The kids constantly made fun of my weight at school too. It was so bad, I never attended my junior or senior prom. Had my dad not made me walk the stage for graduation. I wouldn't have done that either. I was fine with them sending my diploma in the mail.

And my mother is no better and thinks she's not bullying me because she's my mom. It was like I didn't know how to say no or even stand up for myself when it came to her. She knew it too and played off it. The sad part is, I read somewhere that people who are related to you and treat you like shit, feel the same as her. Luna never allowed it to go on too much in front of her and I think its why my mom and her butted heads all the time.

"I love him that much and wanted to do it just so he would be with me."

"Damn Khloe. I'm glad you didn't."

"I love food too much and if him or no other man can't get with these dimples in my legs, cellulite on my thighs and big arms, then fuck em."

"Shit, I'm on the same page. I ain't giving up food for no one and this stomach I got, tells me all the time when it's hungry." She said and bunched it up pretending, it was talking like the crazy girl in White Chicks did in the dressing room.

"Let's get ready." I patted her on the leg and went to get my ringing cell.

"Is everything ok?" I asked Risky.

"Yea. When you coming back? Between your mom and Raina, I don't know who I'm gonna kill first." I could hear how stressed he sounded.

"Why? What happened?" He started telling me how him and Raina were watching television in the living room and my mom stopped by. She went in the kitchen, made her coffee like normal, went back in the living room and changed the channel. Then she had the nerve to tell them, they had their own room with a TV in it. Luna and I were hysterical when he said Raina went in the kitchen, came out and threw a handful of marshmallow at her.

"I'll be home Sunday."

"Be careful out there Khloe."

"I am." He handed the phone to Raina and we sat there talking for over an hour. Once we finished, Luna and I got dressed and were ready to partake in the New York life.

****

"What a fucking weekend." I told Luna as we drove home.

I called Risky and let him know we'd be back around two and try not to kill anyone before I got there. He said Raina was still asleep and my mom wasn't there. He told me if he weren't there, he'd be at the funeral home because someone called in from the hospital asking to get a body. I still don't know how he did that shit.

"Yes bitch, yes. I hope you still have those phone numbers." I nodded my head. We bar hopped the first night, and last night we went to Club Lust. It was mad fun. The strippers were cool as hell and all the guys were buying us drinks and drinking with us. We both met a few guys and promised to stay in touch.

"You better hurry up and get it in before Oscar locks you down." She sucked her teeth."

"Did you tell Waleed about him?"

"I tried but he messed up so there was no need."

"I guess." I opened the car door and stepped out.

"Call me later."

"I will and tell Raina she still owes me a lasagna." I laughed because she told Luna she knew how to make it and it was the best ever. Of course, Luna challenged her and now she's waiting to taste it.

I used my key to open the door, placed my bags on the floor and called out for Raina. Risky's truck wasn't there so I knew he was gone. I went up the steps and knocked on the door. When she didn't answer, I opened it to check on her. She's become my daughter and I found myself even closer to her since the incident.

Her bed was unmade; however, she wasn't in it. I instantly started to panic. It's like my gut was telling something was wrong. I went room to room, looking for her. When I opened the bathroom door my eyes almost popped out my head.

"RAINA NOOOOOO!"

Luna

I dropped Khloe off and drove to my parents' place. I

hadn't seen them since my dad smacked fire from my ass and

twice at that. My mom called and cursed me out. She said,

there's no reason I haven't been there and my dad is an asshole.

If I know my mom, she went in on him and he probably has

showered her with tons of gifts to get back in her good graces.

That's just how he was when it came to my mom.

I pressed the gate and waited for security to open. Once

it did, I drove to the back, parked and went inside. Both of

them were in the kitchen being fresh with one another. I

cleared my throat, put my things down and grabbed something

to drink.

"It's about time you came over. Your father has a few

things he wants to say to you." He came over to me and looked

in my eyes.

"Don't ever talk slick to me again or I'll do more than

smack you."

"Really?" I had my hands on my hips.

"Really? Now." He took a seat on one of the bar stools.

"Your sister has returned but she nowhere to be found." He said with a snarl on his face. When I say my father couldn't stand her, I meant it. If he could've killed her years ago, he would have.

"How is that when I keep running into her ugly ass?" I grabbed a soda out the fridge.

"If you're running into her, it's because she wants you to. I'm sad to report that whoever she's with, has shown her how to stay hidden."

"Ok." I didn't understand where he was going with it.

"Which means, I'm taking your mom away for a while and I want you to come." I tried to protest.

"Just until we find her. Plus, I found out some things about Oscar and his people over in Mexico and I'm not thrilled to say the least."

"What is he planning because I saw him a few days ago at the mall?"

"He's here?" Both of them asked.

"He was but I'm not sure if he's still around."

"Call him and ask where he is." He said.

"Daddy, what is going on?"

"Just do it." I pulled my phone out and dialed his number. I could hear a lot of commotion in the background and then he answered. I placed him on speaker so they could hear.

"What up fat girl?" My mom was livid.

"Fuck you. Where you at? I wanna discuss some things with you about this fake marriage."

"I'm around. Where you tryna meet?"

"We can meet at the soul food place downtown."

"Aight. Give me an hour." I hung up and asked my dad what's next.

"Meet him and leave the rest to me." He rushed out the room and left us standing there. My mom shrugged her shoulders and I glanced down at another threatening message from Waleed. He was really fucking crazy. I did get enjoyment out of it though.

I stayed and talked with my mom for a while and headed to the soul food place. My stomach growled as soon as I pulled up. It was pretty packed but since the lady knew me she gave me a table in the back. I told her a guy would be looking for me when he came in and if she could point him in my direction. I ordered my food and was fucking it up when someone stood in front of my table, blocking my sunlight.

"Why are you here?" I asked and he snatched me up outta my chair.

"You know, I'm beginning to think you're strung out or something. I mean this threatening and stalking shit can't be good for a nigga who sleeps around."

"Your pussy is A fucking 1 Luna but don't get it twisted. There's plenty more bitches out there with some good shit in between their legs."

"Then go bother them." I waved him off and he snatched my wrist.

"I'm tired of playing these fucking games with you. Let's go Luna." He told me to grab my shit and meet him outside. He must be crazy if he thought for one second, I'd go with his looney ass.

"Wale, what you doing over here?" I heard her voice and he let go.

"Really? Get the fuck out my face."

"Let me explain Luna."

"Explain What Waleed? How you keep coming for me but you're out with another bitch? Or how about, me walking into your house where you know I have the key to and watching another woman ride your dick?" I saw his facial expression change. I guess he figured out why I was so mad.

"Or wait, how about finding out you slept with her more than that one night? Which one do you care to explain first?" I wiped my face with a napkin and started grabbing my things. My dad will have to be mad. I'll meet up with Oscar another day. I went to leave and he grabbed my arm as I walked out the door. Him and the bitch followed me.

"WHAT?" I snapped and his face turned to angry.

"Then you parading this bitch in my face. Was all of it a game to you?"

"Is what a game? Luna, you called me and I asked if you slept with someone else. You didn't answer and…"

"And you should've let me finish." He ran his hand down his face.

261

"But instead you fuck the one bitch in the world who has been tryna hurt me since forever."

"What you talking about?" He asked and the bitch stood there grinning.

"Are you serious right now?" Was he really pretending not to know who she was?

"Luna, this is.-" He attempted to speak but I stopped him.

"I know exactly who she is."

"Then who is she?" He had his arms folded, staring at me.

"My fucking sister." That stupid smirk disappeared from his face.

"Hold the fuck up."

"What's the matter Wale? You don't like fucking sisters?" Julie said. I shook my head and let the tears fall. Her face spoke volumes, even if her words didn't. She was happy to see how much hurt he instilled on me.

"You good ma?" Oscar said and I turned around to see him coming closer.

"Who the fuck are you?"

"This is what I was tryna explain to you Waleed."

"Ohhhhh please let me tell him." My sister jumped in front of Waleed and I tried to stop her but Oscar held me back.

"Oscar, this is Wale. Wale, this is Oscar; Luna's husband." I didn't even see him pull the gun out until it was already touching my forehead. If I thought Waleed was gonna kill me before. He was definitely about to kill me now.

To Be Continued...

This book is dedicated to the reader who in boxed me and asked if I could write a book on bullying and suicide. I will not disclose their information, in order to keep them private. I'm not sure if this is happening to the individual but I do hope this book helps or even shows you there are other ways to deal with situations, such as the ones in this story.

I would also like to say, even though this entire book is fiction, Bullying and Suicide is on the rise in America. Kids as young as eight years old are taking their lives and just because it's not happening in your family, doesn't mean it's not going on at all. People tend to turn a blind eye to things not affecting them directly, however; NEVER think it can't happen to you or someone you know.

Cyber, physical, mental, emotional, sexual harassment and so many other ways are signs of bullying. Some may look at it as nothing, while others become depressed, paranoid, threatened, suicidal and etc...

If you or anyone you know has been bullied, or contemplating suicide please talk to someone. You can also contact the suicide hotline. Some may know it and others may not. I listed it down below in case someone needs them.

National Suicide Prevention Hotline

(There is also an online chat if you don't want to speak to someone directly)

1-800-273-8255

Cyber bully Hotline

1-800-420-1479

National Center For Missing and Exploited Children Cyber Tipline

1-800-843-5678

These are just some phone numbers. If you search online, there are a whole lot more.

Made in United States
Orlando, FL
01 August 2022